Whispers
FOR TERRA

Nancy Houser-Bluhm

ISBN: 978-1-7362123-0-1 Paperback

ISBN: 978-1-7362123-1-8 E-book

Whispers for Terra is a work of fiction. Names, characters, places, events,
and incidents are either products of the author's imagination or fictional
composites of past experiences. Any resemblance to actual persons or
events is coincidental. Most names of companies are fictitious but are
referenced in factual ways using common knowledge found online.
All mentions of company employees and communications are fictionalized,
as are all events in the telling of this story. Mentions of actual organizations
or authorities in this book does not imply endorsement by the author, nor
does mention of specific organizations or authorities imply
they endorse this book or its author.

Book Cover Design by Claudia Edwards-Houser

Book Cover Photos by Mo Dedrick

To those in our lives who casually speak the kind words we carry with us

and repeat over and over to ourselves in the moment we most need them.

Terra =
Earth Land Soil

Chapter 1

I DIDN'T KNOW MY WORLD WAS ABOUT TO BE rocked. As I prepared to step into the patient's room, I only knew how my jaw felt as it tightened when I saw the last-minute speech language evaluation order placed at my station. My body had been settling into a feeling of relief for the end of the day. Barbara, a nurse, knew I would be off in ten minutes, but she also knew the policy stated that new evaluations had to be initiated the day they were ordered. Somewhere in me, I knew this wasn't her fault, but I also sensed too much pleasure in it for her, and irritation was an easier emotion for me right now.

As I entered the patient's room, I lifted my head and smiled broadly. As a kid, I was told my smile could light a room. And now, Mr. Talbot would never know I was anything but excited to help him. My soul knew the real story.

I reached for the clipboard and my sleeve slid down. I saw Mr. Talbot look at the mole on my arm, then look questioningly at me. He had no idea the mole had developed over a few short months. I shrugged and gave him a look of "Eh," but my inner self was mirroring his same questioning look. Although most of my patients qualify as elderly and look the frailer part, Mr. Talbot, with his twinkling blue eyes, allowed me to envision the handsomeness he carried when he was younger.

I was relieved to read he was NPO, meaning nothing by mouth, and only tube feeding for now. He'd be safe from the risk of aspirating for the time being; he needed more strength and the medical staff needed more time to put a plan in place. This also made my assessment quick. After screening his language and orientation skills, along with checking the quality of his dry swallow and oral movements needed for chewing and swallowing, I was able to write the evaluation and get out. Grabbing a snack from the break room, I headed down the hall and toward the doors of freedom. My hope of not getting stuck in traffic had been squashed when Barbara placed that evaluation order at my station. While I worked on the evaluation, I thought about all the vehicles that were joining the sea of brake lights on the highway. As I walked out the door, my recurring fantasy kicked in: me running down the hall of Trinity Rehabilitation and Long-Term Care, screaming like a lunatic, "I can't do this anymore!" I thought, *If I have to help one more sick person, I may really find myself screaming in the halls.*

Driving home, I changed from radio station to radio station, finally settling on silence. I found myself conjuring up memories of when I liked talking to people on the phone—vaguely recalling when I used to go out, beyond dragging myself to work. I am not sure when I started the slide from passion to mere competence . I found myself wondering, *Do I look different than before? Can anyone else tell, see it, feel it?* Once home, I watched reruns of *Parks and Recreation*, not caring that I could practically recite the lines. Then my already depressed mind took my meds to squelch any chance of waking before the alarm.

Morning came too soon. The song *Jack Gets Up* began to play, and I had no doubt Leo Kottke wrote that song for me, knowing every morning felt the same. The shower cocooned me, allowing me to avoid the world, and I stood there letting the water nearly singe my skin. The temperature, just on the other side of soothing, reminded me I was alive. I always lingered long after being clean. As the water pelted the back of my neck, I remembered how I used to be kissed there. One of my favorite places. Now, this was the closest I came to that sensation. Eventually, I stepped out, dried off, dressed, and moved on in my robotic way. I was told I was depressed, and a pill could help that. Then it was a stream of pill changes after this reaction or that. I was losing track if I was me before the pills or me after the pills.

•••

I was happy to see Mr. Talbot already looking better when I arrived at work. Beaming with curiosity for people, he started the conversation. "I slept great! Nothing like short-term use of pain meds to reset the sleep clock. How'd you sleep?" he asked me.

"Not bad, but I could use a new bed."

"Do you have a long drive to work?"

"About thirty minutes if I avoid traffic. Just enough to get my head in the game," I said.

"Hard to leave before your kids get off to school?" he asked, clearly fishing for details.

"Well no, I don't have any. My cat is pretty independent. Only myself to drag out of bed." I felt my lips lift to a slight smile in pleasure at my dry humor.

I could see him shifting from patient to person before my eyes. Suddenly, Mr. Talbot wasn't a body in a gown, but he had details: gray hair and strong, thick fingers with knotted joints. This shift was what got me out of bed every day.

"You were a farmer?" I asked.

"I was, but now my garden is only two acres. My wife puts up three hundred cans every year. Nothing like August fruits and vegetables in January."

Barbara came in looking omnipotent in her purpose, with no regard for what I was doing. Her presence implied I was done. She no longer needed words to communicate her power. It pissed me off that I merely responded, and it seemed past time for me to work my way into prominence. She'd gained the control she needed as a passive-aggressive type. I struggled to know how to break the cycle. *My God, I have learned to communicate my truth on so many fronts. Why is this ONE personality type gifted? ... No, why do I gift them the control and find myself*

3

small and slinking away? I am a God damn speech-language pathologist. My career and passion are to help others communicate. On some level, I knew I had only myself to blame. I defer and hand over the lead too easily. It was easier to just resent her.

It started two years ago when I first arrived on the job. Barbara, a tall slender nurse, would walk in silently with meds while I was with a patient. She would greet them and hand them meds without acknowledging me. No "Hello, Mary" or "Excuse me" implied she topped the hierarchy. When I asked her a question, she had minimal eye contact and a slow response time. I was the newbie, never a wave-maker, figured I'd find the right time to say something, or my ever-friendly approach would win her over. Fast-forward these two years, and I reflexively moved back as she moved in.

As she issued medication and listened to Mr. Talbot's heart, I shifted my thinking to getting out early enough today to walk in my woods. I let it occupy my mind. For a couple of minutes, I drifted to the solace I feel from the quiet of the trees and the unassuming lives teeming in the sparsely visited woods.

•••

I got out of my car, changed shoes, and started the trek back to my tree. I knew I couldn't stay long. I heard the breeze whispering of its coming before it arrived, calling a hello to me. It was good to feel it again. The breeze that's free to weave between the swaying trees, not locked among a maze of buildings. The breeze came in waves. I imagined the trees liking it too. A form of body surfing. They saw the wind coming and got ready to ride it.

The tree I'd named Matt came into view. One day, it just came to me that Matt was his name. For me, trees have personalities. Matt's face had given me comfort after Ryan and I split up a couple years ago. Somehow, this face had reassured me I would make it through. His tailored style with bouffant hair and large, warm black eyes were the opposite of what I'd looked at for ten years. About a year ago, I'd scooted a log opposite this tree. I'd sat down and gazed at my friend.

It felt like the first time I had breathed all day. Closing my eyes, I heard a robin's repeating trill, raised then lowered, soothing my mind; the late winter day was fading.

When my mind quieted, it often slipped back to my patients. It was the patients who triggered a reminder of why I loved being a speech-language pathologist. I found they infiltrate my psyche throughout the day. It may be their demeanor, their conversation, or their challenge to get better, which becomes my challenge to help. Reflecting on a conversation with Margaret, a slight but particularly determined woman, I pondered the changes which occur after a stroke. The world changes your trajectory and you find yourself in the fight of your life to retain your personal power. You long for these new people standing before you to see who you are, not just what the stroke has left behind. The you before only part of your body worked and before your energy was exhausted by simple acts, even eating. Families want to alleviate the worry and provide comfort. First, they start doing for you or talking for you, and then too often, deciding for you. With just the shift of the clock from one second to the next, your world can be changed, as it was for Margaret.

Margaret spoke with kindness and a gentle understanding for people. She could make me laugh with her witty quips. She explained what I saw before me was not who she was. I told her, "Margaret, I can see your spirit shining through." She responded, "That's God's spirit." It was a calling I had answered. I'd always liked old people. If they'd gotten through so many years with grace and beauty, then I needed to learn their secret.

If I saw my job as one where I washed an aging body … cooked for an aging body … walked an aging body, then it would be hard to find meaning in why I showed up for work. If I understood I was helping a soul in an aging body retain dignity, honor, and worth, then I also gained dignity for myself. That is when this work becomes a calling, not somewhere I go so I can have health insurance and vacation time.

Chapter 2

I WOKE UP SO REFRESHED. FRESH AIR OFTEN LED to solid sleep. Since I had time at home before working a midday shift, I had a chance to get on my bike trainer and ride. I noticed my iPod lying on the shelf. *Geez, I wonder if it still works?* I was struggling to recall how the archaic piece of equipment even turned on. Once I did, I found my first-ever playlist full of rhythmic spinning speed songs. iPods were the coolest thing. The bike dancing kicked in, and I drummed my arms, bobbed my head, rolled my shoulders, and moved to the beat, infused with the song's energy and bursting out the lyrics that reflected me. Three songs on my playlist had undoubtedly been written when they heard my cries. Katy Perry's *Firework*, Sara Bareilles's *Brave*, and Cimorelli's *Believe It*. These songs gave me hope when my world crashed. Olympic Gold Medalist Scott Hamilton warmed up to the *Rocky* theme song. I merely dreamed to speak my truth, find my voice, not necessarily be recognized for it. To feel brave instead of fearful.

As I was cocooning in my shower chrysalis, I realized how quickly this new mole had become part of me. I didn't mind it, although I knew if it was on one of my patients, I'd shame them into getting it checked out. It didn't have the markings of cancerous moles—black, irregular. It was oval, smooth, about dime-size. It was just new and sudden.

As I walked in to work, I told myself I would love this day. I knew a later shift was good for my body. Work was humming and the rehab wing was full. I was swamped but could handle it today. Walking down the hall, I heard, "Yoohoo, yooohoo," spoken with a sweet melody as I passed a room. Looking at the name tag on the door, I walked in.

"Hi Lena, my name is Mary, is there something you need?" She was blind and somewhat hard of hearing. She wanted water, and it wasn't in reach. I offered her the glass and then placed it on the tray table and oriented her to its placement.

"Can you stay a few minutes? The nice OT was in helping me get cleaned up, but it was more business than talking. I have to focus so much on not bending too far, and using the equipment takes all my concentration." She was talking about Laurie, the occupational therapist. *Laurie was so caring, quick to laugh, and always ready for a party. I needed to open myself up to a good time. It'd been too long since my breath was cut off with laughter.*

"Lena, what brings you in here?"

"I know every inch of my apartment, but a nice repairman was in on Monday and moved my trash can. I knocked right into it, fell and broke this old hip and a rib. Lucky that's all it was." I discovered I wasn't destined to get to know her. A ninety-seven-year-old woman living alone, whether or not she should have been, but she could talk, swallow, and knew the date. Not a speech patient.

Holding her audience, she asked, "How's your day going?"

I replied, "It's a good one but it's just begun. Let's hope it can stay that way."

Lena lay silent for a moment then said, "What are you worried about? Your day can be whatever you want it to be." *I wish I was better at framing it that way.*

I had to move on, but I could tell I'd be back to talk with her. I was so inspired by my octogenarians and nonagenarians. I didn't know if it was good or bad, but my generation seemed to focus on all our shit more than her generation did. They appeared to have either sucked it up or taken things in stride, not expecting all days to be roses and tulips.

7

I ran into Laurie in the rehab office, told her I'd met Lena, and found myself asking if she might be able to stop for a drink after work one day soon. It'd been too long. "Yay, the lemon drop shots queen is reviving," she giggled. Laurie had been a friend for years and was the one who got me to shift jobs to Trinity. Always finding the positive, she was a steady force after Ryan left, when I was adjusting to the unanticipated single life.

I thought about Lena off and on much of the day. She didn't worry about her thin gray hair or crepe paper skin. I'd be so pissed if I was blind and hard of hearing. Her response to not being able see or hear when someone was passing by was to beckon them with a melody that wraps them with warmth. Over the next couple of weeks, I found myself stopping by at least once a day. She was only expecting to be here a couple weeks for the hip, but returning home was being questioned. After a few days, I started taking my lunch in her room, even though I should have gotten fresh air or done paperwork. Lena was lucky enough to have a room with a window view of the back courtyard full of trees and a bird feeder, but it was lost because she didn't know it and couldn't hear the chirps and flits of the wings in takeoff. She wasn't deaf but the subtle sounds went unnoticed.

Turning her head toward the window, she said, "Tell me what you see out there, will you?"

"Your room backs up to our back courtyard. There are aspens and pine. There's a bird feeder hanging from the eave out your window. Right now, there are five birds vying for the food."

"What else, are there any faces?"

"No, no one is out there right now, it's a cool day."

"No, not people, nature faces?" I felt a pinch in my mind, and my eyes darted to her.

"You mean faces on the trees? Have you seen them, Lena?"

"Oh my, I used to all the time." Tilting her head, she said, "I am thinking you know what I mean."

I noticed I was holding my breath. "Yes, I do see faces in nature, all the time. I just don't talk much about them. When I do speak of them, people don't see what I see. I have to draw it out for them, but the faces are almost alive for me."

"Merely because someone else doesn't see them, doesn't mean they aren't there, or that you should stop talking about them. Your silence robs them of the gift of the real you."

Lena couldn't see my slouched shoulders as I replied, "I have never worn the badge of anomaly very well."

"Anomalies can be an inspiration for others. Have you always seen them, the faces?"

I replied, "I can remember tending my parents' garden. I'd see life moving on the soil as an entire world of tiny beings, viewing me as the local giant. I don't recall the first tree face I ever saw."

When I stood, I felt a little taller, and my eyes glinted with a hope I was yet to understand. "Lunch is over, but you have given me something to ponder."

●●●

After work, Laurie and I stopped at Bony's for a beer and fish tacos. There are no secrets of the body with an OT. We laughed, telling fun stories of patients, but always honoring them. Even watching tattoos collapse on a patient's aging skin didn't stop Laurie from having her own. No one stays working in geriatrics long without having an innate love for each person's life story or their continued zest for life that people of our generation can easily lose track of. Conversation switched to family drama and hopes for the future.

I didn't have much to add when she asked, "Have you dated anyone?" I shook my head. She said, "Mary, Ryan wasn't that great to begin with. Yeah, you got screwed in the settlement, but honey, it's been over two years." I found myself pondering that length of time during my drive home. I needed to reconnect with the me I wanted to be before I let it get muddied with other influences.

I knew I would sleep well. I had enough real drugs to make that happen. I'd had some level of insomnia for years, from either work or relationship anxiety, rehashing events, or what-I-wish-I-had-said scenarios. Tonight, seeing a glimpse of my old self, it would be a different sleep. The kind that heals the body and gives it strength. If I was lucky, I'd have a good dream I'd remember. Not one where I was lost, or trying to find my way through the maze of halls just wanting to get outside to my car, or the one in which I was feeling overlooked, or a guy I was dating in my dream morphed into my ex. Not that one, either.

It turned out that in my dream, I was in the old house of my parents' friend, but it was a nursing home now. My dad was living there. He only stared into space, and Vera kept saying, "No, no" and beckoning forward with her hands for him to look at her. He would look and smile. Each time she did this, he'd momentarily transform to a more youthful man of forty-five. They would connect, old friends seeing each other for who they remembered, and then actually returning to who they remembered.

I woke up from that dream so gratified that I had gotten to see my dad, who passed away four years ago. I was particularly warmed by seeing him as the young man I could only recall from pictures. I knew from Jeremy Taylor, a dream interpretation guru, that all our dream characters are some pieces of ourselves. Having a few minutes before I actually had to put feet to the floor, I reconnected to the dream. Vera was vibrant, confident, ageless. Vera's oldest daughter was my best friend in grade school. Laughter and banter always filled their home. My dad was ill for the last two years of his life, with his life force seeping from his declining heart. The meaning here was no big surprise, was it? Vera was the me I had hoped to age like. My dad was me now, with life force seeping away. I could have seen it as me being Vera, beckoning the best from my patients, but why analyze dreams at all, if I am going to avoid the truth.

While wrapped in the warmth of the shower, I let myself bask in the joy of seeing my dad healthy and smiling. I resembled him with my long nose and dark, almost black hair. I left for work feeling lifted by connecting with Laurie last night and now having connected with Dad. I could focus on the purpose of the dream's underlayment another time.

Chapter 3

B ARBARA WAS IN A GRACIOUS MOOD TODAY. I gave her my schedule, and she didn't seem to object to any of it. I knew the rehab department drove the profits for this place, but there was still a hierarchy of command that I allowed to perpetuate. It wasn't that she didn't do her job well; God only knows the life-and-death responsibilities of a nurse would keep me up at night. So did the impact of dysphagia, swallowing disorders, one of the deficits my patients sometimes experienced after a stroke or other neurological events. I learned after a couple early blunders to recommend the absolute safest diet texture and that demonstrating the swallowing strategies clearly to the CNAs kept the patients safe and allowed me to sleep at night. This would keep the waking dreams at bay. The one in which I wake at 2:00 a.m. watching myself get sued and sent to jail. ... Dysphagia was only on the horizon when I entered speech pathology, but it was now a driving force of the caseload in skilled nursing.

I knew one of my life lessons was to learn to operate on equal terms with the passive-aggressive personality type. Every job change had brought a sense of relief to not be working with THAT person anymore, and the next thing I knew, they appeared in another body; sometimes they were female, sometimes male, sometimes a colleague, sometimes a boss. I would vow that this time, it'd be different, but then one day I'd realize I'd acquiesced and given away my own power. On this job, it was Barbara. It bothered me more than it did others but caused a perfect storm with a collision of her passive-aggressive personality and my avoidance of conflict. I learned it takes more energy to circumvent the person than to be direct, but once entrenched, the realignment seems too much.

I had lunch with the team that day. Once a week, we'd go to a nearby amphitheater and bask in the warmth and fresh air, getting away from the scent that lingered from the facility. We'd watch others as they climbed stairs and ran patterns through the venue. I found myself missing lunch with Lena. I'd be sure to see her tomorrow.

•••

I was lucky to have the woods right outside my apartment, even luckier no one else seemed interested in them. The forest floor was the same. Nothing was disturbed from other footprints. I was a looker-downer. For whatever reason, I walked with my head down, and I had to remind myself, to force myself, to gaze at the sky and the growing leaves. I could tell you almost whatever you wanted to know about the trail and vegetation. I connected to the dirt, to the energy from the ground.

I got to my log and sat for a time. Matt was there as a sentry to my path. As I closed my eyes, letting go of the day, I heard a woodpecker's tap tap and the skwaack of a crow. Opening my eyes, I gazed at an ant working to carry a piece of leaf home. That was when I heard it coming from far away, the wind, and realized a blast of wind was working its way through the trees, causing everything along the way to silence and brace. It slammed my back, pushing me forward so that I had to hold the log to stay on it. The wind rushed past Matt, causing his home to bend. I heard cracks as some dead branches fell to the ground. It was gone, I could hear it move on, and stillness returned. *What the hell was that!?* I found myself noticing other trees and for a flash, saw sparks among them. Not fire sparks, light sparks being released as if fireflies had been born from them. They traveled from one tree to the next, intermixing. Then they were gone. I tried to recapture the experience, but whatever the wind brought forth was over.

My mole felt warm. Comforting warm, not sickly warm. Why wasn't this thing alarming me? It made no sense. It had quickly become a part of me. As much a part as these small woods, which were a holdout of nature in the gradually encroaching town. I left those woods feeling a sense of strength.

•••

I made it a point to see Lena the next day for lunch. Her blindness didn't seem to confine her real vision. She saw into me, seeing my soul. Lena reached out for my hand, and I moved forward to meet hers. She gave a little squeeze and relaxed into a gentle caress. Her other hand reached over and ran down my forearm. She could feel the mole through the light shirt fabric. She felt its smoothness and slowly, lightly, rubbed her index finger back and forth over it, then tracing it.

It was calming, reassuring, and I suddenly felt more okay with who I was. With a trance-like stare out the window, I knew Ryan's leaving me wasn't my problem. I'd always known it in my head, but I was sensing its truth in my very cells. I knew I couldn't continue to be the strong exterior but fearful interior I lived in. Simultaneously, I knew I would talk with Barbara, but I also knew bigger things.

"Tell me about the other faces you see," Lena suddenly asked, jarring me back to the room.

"My faces aren't all permanent. Some are formed from the snow piles on the branches, causing a droop that creates their kindness, or pine needles forming luscious eyelashes. Some are male, some female. They look so different but all kind and gentle. All comforting, curiously friendly. Even the ones with gruffness are very clearly protective," I answered.

"Why do you think you see them when others, so many others, don't?"

"My mom always referenced my overactive imagination."

"I don't think you are as alone with this as you may think," Lena said. "Sometimes you just have to find the right people."

Hmmmm, no coincidences just like in The Celestine Prophecy. We ate the rest of our lunch in silence. I felt the warmth of the sun from the window as I pondered.

Chapter 4

I HAD TO PREP FOR A REHAB COOKING GROUP with Laurie. She focused on the patients' fine motor skills and the activities of daily living embedded in each part of the cooking process. I focused on reading, following the sequence of the cooking process, and their attention to details. We both watched the safety closely, not only for our liability but ultimately to help determine readiness for cooking at home.

One of our ladies was an outgoing woman who wanted to demonstrate a specialty of hers, quesadillas. She was chefing it up perfectly, but cooking on someone else's stove is always risky, and the final process resulted in smoke. A lot of smoke. There was no risk of fire, but smoke was billowing throughout the kitchen by the time we thought to open the windows. The fire alarm sounded. We were able to alert administration that we were the source so evacuation could be circumvented, but the fire department was on their way. No turning back from that one. But oh, we decided the embarrassment was worth the beauty we beheld in these tall, young men in full rescue gear coming through the door. "Has there ever been an ugly firefighter?" one patient asked. Being all women, and some over eighty, they giggled like teenagers, and Laurie and I joined in. We reflected on the sight of the men using much of the height of the door as they entered the haze of smoke.

The rest of the day went more smoothly and was less stressful than most. It occurred to me that relaxing with Lena was setting the stage for a good second half of the day. I typically did paperwork as I mindlessly crammed in an apple and a sandwich.

I was getting ready to wrap things up for the day when I saw Bob walking in. Patients like him are the best perk of the job. He was an independent man. Being only in his early seventies, he was young compared to so many of my patients who had suffered a stroke. He was able to communicate fine, but his cognitive endurance, reasoning, and concentration for such key tasks as driving were impacted. We'd worked together during his rehab stay on tasks requiring a progressively longer attention span and more detail, more ingenuity to figure out the answers. Bob smiled hugely when he saw me coming, and I gave him a bear hug when we met. "How's my favorite little brain-picker?" he chuckled. I was not sure I'd ever had such a high compliment. He told me proudly that he'd driven himself that day. He'd come to pick up a few items that had been in the laundry when he was discharged. "I sure wasn't gonna wait around for them and have someone change their mind!" he said.

Initially, my work with Bob had been mentally fatiguing and equally frustrating for him. It takes a strong person to fail miserably in front of someone young enough to be your daughter and then also have to accept feedback from a person you should be giving it to. I rarely risked it myself. But Bob had persevered, and his hard work paid off, later able to tell people he'd had a near, if not full, recovery.

I left rejuvenated, re-establishing my sense of value and purpose. Speech pathology, the science and art for improving the ability to communicate, was absolutely my calling. I didn't realize how a series of events had set me up for this work. My own difficulty being understood up to first grade, and years later, seeing my kindergarten report card that said I didn't even speak in complete sentences. Having peers slightly older prod me into saying something they knew I would mispronounce, so they could laugh. Meeting Tricia in high school, and seeing how people innocently assumed she was cognitively impaired due to her communication disability, and not giving her a chance to use her skills. They weren't being mean. Their own uncomfortableness with her presence caused them to assume and do everything for her.

Bob probably didn't know how much my psyche needed his reminder of our work these days. This had been a fun day where I felt on top of my game, not struggling to look as if I was enjoying the art of having to motivate another patient.

I left and headed home. Traffic didn't even daunt me. With the window open, my long hair was blowing wildly in the wind. Usually I stared ahead, tight-lipped, warning other drivers to pay more fucking attention next time. *How about planning a merge? Using your fucking turn signal is always a good idea.* Today, I waved them in with a smile.

God, the universe loved me today. Lunch with Lena, sexy firemen, Bob, pleasing drive, and energy for a salad with protein versus microwaving a mac and cheese. I needed to recapture that day! Tequila jumped onto my lap, hoping to lap up the last of the grapeseed oil on my plate. Her name made me smirk. At eight years old, she was a testimony of my party life and what seemed to be a lifetime ago.

I still didn't trust much since those days. It's called baggage, this stuff I carry around. "She's got too much baggage." We were just learning about PTSD in those days. We didn't know that when the brain perceives a similar situation is being set up, even though it isn't, the body zip-lines into full response mode. The response is visceral, and logic seems out of reach. My trigger: late people. I have never seen much reason to be late, and an hour, maybe three, probably meant I wasn't important enough or someone was up to no good. Turns out, that described Ryan.

I scanned through the channels, hoping to find a feel-good story to keep my groove going. *Ah, this is interesting … is there really a third eye?* I'd heard the term. In yoga, the teacher would ask us to balance with our eyes closed, seeing the focus spot with our third eye. I had never succeeded in that one. The third eye was one of our chakras; I knew that. It was supposed to see the world as it really existed, not only what was solid before us. I had read so many self-help books and spiritual guidebooks. Maybe I always felt a hole in my spirit as if I was supposed to have a gift but didn't. A void or loneliness I couldn't explain. Auras, Reiki, on and on. I was what I called a spiritual dabbler, master of none. Skip a couple decades and here I was. Dream-work could be the single thing I stuck with while others faded at the least sign of resistance. Part of me wanted to have expertise, while another part of me doubted the potential, or even more, feared it. I feared the learning curve, feared the failure, feared the commitment, while a little part whispered, *I could be more*. In hindsight, I was hoping a gift would reveal itself with little or no work involved.

Pulling out the old dabbler experience, I drank some water before bed and asked the universe for a dream, a great one. Some sex would be ideal. I acknowledged I didn't feel the need for my sleep pill. I felt tired and just GOOD. I didn't say that very often. Typically, I knew when it was time to take the pill. Surely, for a time, one pill or another had been too close of a friend. I was at a bar with a group of women one night a couple years back and was shocked when I heard how many of us were taking some mood-altering medication. Couldn't we be happy with what we had going in life? No kids, too many kids, no partner, no dates, no job, too much job stress, boredom. It was hard to know if expectations for the happiness meter changed over the years or if people were just dealing with it differently now, compared to decades ago. It was kind of like PTSD. Mental health was finally in the forefront of society's awareness versus under some family rug or in their closet. I thought, *No matter how I accomplish a good night's sleep, it's good night world.*

Chapter 5

MY FIRST WAKING THOUGHT WAS THAT IT WAS my day off since I would be working the weekend round. I never minded working on the weekend. The unit was calmer, quieter, and I got to document that a patient or two was out with family. That morning, I decided on a longer hike, but first, coffee. I loved when I could sip my coffee slowly rather than gulp it as I go out the door or scald my tongue in the car.

Tequila lounged in the sun that was framing my lap while I sipped. Her quest to firmly nuzzle her head on any edge always meant I needed to hold the cup firmly as she nuzzled. She'd lick my fingers if they carried the scent of coconut oil from adding it to my coffee. Today, she seemed enamored with my mole. Rubbing her ear on it, sniffing around it, rubbing some more.

Entering the woods, I recognized I was lucky to have this serene place, designated a wilderness area. It was not an advertised state park or anything that would bring droves of people. I passed by Matt, my sentry, and waved hello with a silent, "I'll be back this way." I hiked farther in than I usually got to go after a long day of work. I could hear coyotes yipping in their pack. I knew they didn't want me; they were just honoring their day. Maybe they caught a sizable rabbit to share. I pictured one of the nature shows I love, recalling how I leave the room or switch channels just before the predator catches their prey. I know it's a natural circle of life; I don't want to witness it firsthand.

•••

I was walking my usual way, looking down at the path two feet ahead, when I almost stumbled into a decaying log. It had fallen recently; I could tell it hadn't been lying there long. The leaves and twigs around it looked freshly disturbed. Maybe it fell during that wind cyclone that came through the other day. I looked up, seeing the trunk it'd fallen from just on the other side of the path. My gaze was drawn back to the downed portion by the face looking up at me. He was obviously no youngster of a tree, looking worn as if he'd seen many battles. He reminded me of some character out of *Braveheart*, not as pretty as the warriors in *Outlander*. His long, oval face had one downturned eye like Hugh Grant and a patch over the other. The eyebrow was a bushy zigzag. A stubby round nose and a lower jaw covered with a scraggly mustache and beard shielding his mouth and chin from the elements. I etched Warrior Man's face in my mind and walked on a bit farther.

I was so timid with some aspects of my life, but the woods emboldened me. I knew women who never walked the woods alone; it's where crazies and rapists lurk. I felt emotionally safer among the trees than in the city and, in some ways, at work. I may have been most guarded at work, but I felt protected by the wood faces I saw in the forest. Those same ones I had to point out to other people. I had never been hurt by the woods, never minimized or shamed. The tower of trees and welcoming foliage embraced me. I was never alone. I decided to go off-path. It was a wild hair.

I had to step over fallen branches and through some brambles. After about a hundred yards, I saw a cairn built from stones. I hesitated, realizing I was not the only off-path traveler in these woods. My bravery came into question, and I turned around. Maybe another day. I backtracked about twenty-five yards and decided the cairn had looked as if it'd been there awhile. I turned back, more curious than worried. Another hundred yards or so, I saw another, but this wasn't stacked; its stones were laid out in the shape of an arrow pointing to the left. *Was I being stupid?* I always carried my car keys since my apartment key was on them. I pictured that old college trick of fighting off an attacker by placing each key strategically between my fingers, apparently mirroring the idea of brass knuckles.

I veered left and not much farther, I came upon a lean-to. It was made from what was probably downed branches with moss and smaller branches for a top. No other sign of an inhabitant but obviously human-made. I sat under it for a few minutes and looked out and up to see what a person would see from that perspective. *Whoa.* A suspended rope ladder leading to a thick branch with a hallowed area. A perfect perch. The rope started about three feet off the ground, so a person would need some climbing skills to get to the first foothold. *I might need different shoes to attempt that.* Feeling a wee edgy, I decided to head back to my Warrior tree. *When I return, I will need to be sensible and carry more than my keys.* As was my common practice, I stopped and added a couple of stones to the existing cairn. I said my goodbyes to Warrior Man and Bouffant Matt and made my way back home.

Since it was Friday, I thought I'd see if someone was available for dinner and a drink. I acknowledged that I was considering going out twice in a couple weeks, and I wondered if a shift was happening. Kelly was happy to meet up. We always had great conversations, and she was the least inclined to think my new-aged ideas were loony. Every time we chatted, I felt a lift. Both raised Catholic, neither of us felt at home in their archaic doctrines about women, and we could mutually laugh, remembering the ol' venial sins. We knew the doctrines had updated, just not enough for us.

We started there, and I shifted to reincarnation. "I never understood how a benevolent God could send someone to hell for eternity, when in contrast, they were bad for a few decades. Sounds like one more way to control patrons." Kelly replied, "Let's have another drink and toast to having another turn to get it right!" "Sure!" I answered. "After all, we Ubered so we can have a bit too much."

I told her about my walks in the woods and finding the lean-to. She rushed out an, "I would have freaked out and probably would have run-not-walked out of there."

"I guess I was more intrigued than scared. I wonder if it's a homeless person. I rarely see others out there, but it took some care to build the structure." Gazing off dreamily, I continued, "That ladder, not sure what it was there for, but maybe it leads to a spot like an easy chair."

Kelly paused, shifting to, "So I am dating a new guy. Met him online and we have been hanging out a couple months." She chuckled and added, "Officially dating, I guess. So far, he doesn't seem to be Ted Bundy."

"Ooooh, what's he look like, do for a living, what does he like to do? Do tell." *May as well live vicariously, my life is pretty freaking dry.*

"His name is Rhett and it feels so nice to look forward to spending time together. It took quite a while to get here. Remember some of those epic date fails, like the bald guy that had the profile picture of a man forty pounds thinner and a full head of hair, or the guy who was in the restaurant business but was the dishwasher? Well, Rhett is a science teacher at Carter Middle School. He loves the age group. He's five feet nine, blond, funky glasses, which I always like, and a bit pudgy but who am I to talk. He likes to read, does some hiking. Maybe we could walk your beloved woods with you one day!"

As I was listening, I envisioned walking behind them and that I'd be thinking how sweet they looked holding hands, him towering over her five-foot slender frame. She only perceived herself overweight. Someone in her past probably told her that.

"I'd love to meet him, and I'd love to show you around. Maybe you could hike to the lean-to with me. It may make more sense going in force."

"It's a date."

We decided we needed to head home and made a plan for a couple weekends out. I always felt alive after being with Kelly. She brought an energy I would have loved to carry with me. In fact, I did carry it with me for a few hours after seeing her. Kind of Pig-Pen's dust cloud but a happy aura that infuses in mine for a while.

I got home and found myself thinking about Lena, along with all the old people I see. Long-term care is like a microcosm of any town. Some people are happy and choose to be where they are. Others make the best of the situation, and others fight it every inch of the way, destined to be miserable. Most eighty- and ninety-somethings grew up treating the earth well, partly because they didn't know any other way. Many "advances" weren't thought up until after WWII. Then their understanding of the earth became the outdated ways of grandmas and grandpas who needed to move over to make way for technology.

Feeling Kelly's positive energy, along with a couple drinks under my belt, I decided tomorrow would be the day I would approach Barbara. *I have let this perpetuate too long. I need to tell her my concerns about how we operate.* I wrote down my issues. I remember once in counseling being told to put in at least one positive after every couple of problems. *Positive – when I see you in the break room with people, everything is more relaxed, and I find you easier to talk with. Problem – when we are on the floor, I feel like the things I ask are put on the back burner ... as if I am not as important as other people. I try not to interrupt as you are measuring/counting pills, etc., so I let you know I need something. Problem – I know a nurse's pace is crazy, but I find I avoid telling you important things because they will be dismissed anyway, or you aren't really listening. Positive – you are a dedicated nurse and I understand the amount of focus your job requires and the frequency of interruptions, but I am frustrated with feeling dismissed.*

I wasn't sure if this was the best way to do it all, but it was a start and we'd see where it went. The challenge would be in finding the time and place to get her to focus on me. Maybe with it being a weekend day, it would all move more slowly and there'd be more time. I took my sleep aid, and surprisingly, I fell asleep in minutes.

I woke up feeling pretty refreshed, ready to take it on. Decided to eat my breakfast of champions: an English muffin with almond butter and blueberry preserves. I scrolled through my iPod to Sara B's *Brave* and listened to the words of the power song.

Can I take Sara with me when I talk to Barbara? Have her words loop in my ear and inspire me to stand my ground, not slink. Own my words, not doubt them.

I got to work and, looking at the schedule, realized several of my patients would be out with family for much of the afternoon. Barbara was already working her rounds. I observed for a bit to watch for my "in" (without appearing to look weird) in between med passes and patient checks. *Now.*

"Hey Barbara, I'd love to talk to you about something today but want you to have five or ten minutes. Any idea when that might be?"

"What about?"

"Just want to share some thoughts with you. Get your thinking on it."

"I was about ready to go on break. How about in five minutes?"

Oh crap. Expected to have more time to ruminate, rehearse, and maybe secretly was hoping the time wouldn't present itself. "Sure! Thanks! How about at the picnic table in the courtyard?"

"Well now I am curious," she added.

I wish I had Googled how to interact with the "passive-aggressive" personality type. I could be going about this all wrong. Barbara was outside smoking. *At least she will be relaxed having had her ciggy.* I took in her tightly curled, salt-and-pepper hair. *Let's do this, Mary.*

Sitting across from her at the table, I looked at her momentarily, wondering if she noticed my hard swallow as I was finding my words. "Barbara, we have had some good chatter in the break room, but I am really frustrated about our on-the-floor interactions."

"What do you mean frustrated? Why?"

"I feel when I approach you in the hall about something I need, you barely look at me, dismiss my request, and I have to come back several times."

"I am busy you know."

"I understand there's a window when things need to get done, but it makes me feel what I need is not important. I am quite busy myself with needing to meet 90 percent productivity every day. This gets tracked too. I get called out if I am below expected productivity more than occasionally."

"What do you want, for me to stop everything because you walked up?"

I tried to remember my planned conversation. "That's a good question, what do I want? I want you to be aware that when I walk up to you, it's because I truly need something or to update you on a patient's safety, not because I am just being a self-centered SLP." After a pause, "I guess I want you to acknowledge me and if you can't get to it right away, then ask me to come back in two minutes, or actually remember to check with me. Chances are, I am still with that patient. When you come in and I am with a patient, I feel you silently cue that my time is over, but our session may not be finished. I give you my schedule and, like I said, I, too, am held accountable for my time."

She begrudgingly said, "I will try to keep that in mind but can't make any promises."

"Barbara, I am not trying to offend you." *Oh yes, a positive.* "Just want things to shift a bit."

"I have to get back inside, as I said, I will try to keep it in mind."

Alrighty. Not exactly the response I was hoping for. Hoping more for a revelation on her part, even fantasized a "I had no idea I was doing this!" but that didn't happen. At least I opened the door. It will continue to be on me to barge through the proverbial door versus walking away meekly. Ugh, hope I don't really need anything from her today. That will be particularly awkward.

●●●

After that, my nerves needed my Lena fix. I popped in and said hi. She informed me she would be starting to go to the dining room for meals.

She appeared only marginally excited at the prospect. "I suppose the food may be warmer coming straight from the kitchen, but one place pretty much looks like another to me." She smiled wryly after she said it, but it struck me what that must feel like. I replied, "You seem to see better than many sighted people."

While in the dining room, I saw her sitting with others. Since everyone was somewhere on the hearing-loss spectrum, conversation was pretty stilted. I realized I might need to find another time for us to sit, maybe after work, since her eating at the standard lunch time was my busy time working with patients on their swallowing strategies. I was hoping the smell of cooking food would appeal to her. Sometimes, the sight of it was not as good as the smell. It had certainly improved, though, with the recent arrival of a new chef.

Luckily, my day whizzed by smoothly, and I didn't have to interact with Barbara. *Whew.* I knew traffic wouldn't be an issue on a Saturday and was able to stop in to the dining room and sit with Lena for a few minutes before going. She cut right to the chase.

"Are you married or have a man?"

"Neither." Then I quickly added, "Why? Do you have an eligible grandson?"

Ignoring my clever response, she asked, "Are you lonely? Do you live alone?"

"Mostly, and yes."

Funny, when elderly people ask a question that I'd be pissed to get from other people, I just accept it, and even more, I find myself answering it.

Deflecting, I asked her about her life. After all, she's ninety-seven years old. There must be a story there.

"Were you married?"

"Oh yes, for fifty years. I have been without Harold for twenty-five years."

"Wow. That's a lot of years. Seems everything would meld and you'd forget how to go it alone."

With a strong nod, she confirmed, "There is a horrific adjustment. Even in the imperfect marriage, love morphs into comfortable love, and the struggles are carried with you as wisdom. And when you suddenly watch yourself foggily moving through the day after all the mourners have returned to their lives, you get hit with a sense of loss that only time navigates."

"Sounds like an old song, *Ghost in This House* by Alison Krauss. You could have written that song."

She said softly, "Eventually, you recognize yourself and begin to know the person wasn't a saint, but he was your imperfect. You miss him every day for years, but you start seeing the world around you again."

"When did you start to go blind?"

The CNA was taking residents back to their rooms. My question had to wait.

"Now there's a story for the days ahead. You need to hear it one day soon."

Chapter 6

IT WAS STILL LIGHT WHEN I GOT HOME, so I thought I'd go say hi to my friends in the woods. I wasn't spending every evening cruising through all the TV channels. I realized I was spending more days and longer periods in my woods.

I walked back to the Warrior and thanked him for watching me thus far. *Am I crazy for talking to these trees? What is friendship, after all? Energy among things that gives you a sense of value, purpose? I suppose friends lead you to a sense of self-acceptance.*

I veered off at the downed log, watching for the cairn. Jerking to a stop, I was surprised when I saw two more stones added to the stack. *Shit. I am not the only one who passes this way. Is it a warning, a "hey," or an enticing welcome?* I looked around but only saw the woods. I didn't feel watched but needed to think about what I should do. *Don't be stupid. God only knows it could be a trap.* I found my mind thinking of those who worry that the woods are a place for weirdos and rapists.

I turned around, giving myself time but knowing I would be back. *Maybe someone is just as curious about who else is in "their" woods as I am. Or they are banking on my curiosity and it's a great way to entice me? Oh, the life of the paranoid mind gets aggravating. How many things have I passed up? Do I follow my head or my gut?*

Cutting it short in the woods, I made it home in time to course through the TV channels. I noticed it wasn't feeling as if I was doing it with the usual desperation. This time, it was more about filling the conscious gap while my brain processed what I saw. Still deciding which side of my paranoid line was the strongest.

I jumped as a knock at the door interrupted my dazed thinking. In the two years I had lived there, it'd only take a hand with a finger or two amputated to count the number of times someone had knocked on that door. I opened it up to see a boy with large brown eyes and straight brownish hair. I recognized him as living in my complex, having noticed him playing out back occasionally, seemingly building small houses from twigs. He hadn't lived there a full year, though. I guessed he was about ten. He was holding an envelope and a pen, and I realized, *Oh boy, school fundraiser time.*

"Hi, I live upstairs and we are selling magazines for my fifth grade field trip."

"Where will you be going?"

"The class is going to Waves Water Park, but people who sell $150 get to spend the night at the zoo. We get to ride there in a limo!"

Even though my explanation was lost on him, I said, "I'll look, but there isn't much that usually attracts my attention enough to get it for an entire year, especially when I get email offers for the next five years."

Stepping outside my door, I slid down the wall to the floor and started looking through the brochure. *I like biking but am not that avid. I like cooking but don't need a bunch of recipes for eight when there's only one.* My eyes stopped at one called *New Age.* Intrigued, I noticed the price was low, only six deliveries a year. *Won't be filling landfills with this one.*

"I'll take this one."

His eyes brimmed with tears, and I was taken back at the value of my words to him. He silently handed me the order form, and I saw that I was the first entry on the page.

"Am I your first door?"

"Tenth."

"Geez, you have fortitude."

"Some people don't even come to the door. I know they are home; I can hear the TV. Not sure if that is better or worse than just telling me no."

"Ya know, I work in a place with a lot of people. They are always putting their kids' fundraiser forms in the lounge. Candy, popcorn, storage containers. I could take yours to work for a day and encourage people to buy. My name is Mary, what's yours?"

"Matt."

"Do you think you should ask your mom first?"

"Well, I don't live with my mom. I live upstairs for now. I am in foster care. Most kids that get the big orders talk about having grandmas, grandpas, aunts, uncles, and neighbors that buy from them. They don't even step out to ask. Their mom does the work."

I tried to hide my sympathetic look but at the same time I felt a warmth arcing between us as I handed him the pen.

"Can I have it till Monday? There won't be as many people at work tomorrow since it's Sunday. Come back Monday. When do you need to turn it in?"

"Friday." He beamed. "Thanks. What does fortitude mean?"

"Fortitude. In my mind it means not easily giving up, believing the next try will be better. Yours just paid off."

I shut off the TV and stared at the form for a bit, feeling an odd sense of pleasure. I so love my elder folk, but it felt vitalizing to talk to someone under sixty-five. To look at a face that wasn't full of lifelines and worry about their changed path stemming from a body-ravishing health issue. I went to bed early and felt as if it'd be a good night's sleep. *Hmmm, a couple of those lately.* When I woke up, I hopped in the shower and enjoyed the warmth and steam but later recognized I didn't need to convince myself to turn off the water.

When I got to work, I wrote a note to staff on a piece of colored paper, gently explaining who the boy was and why it was important to consider getting just one magazine. I did add the enticement of mini candy bars. "Feel free to take a couple for every magazine ordered," and a smiley face. Matt only needed twenty names to get the zoo trip. Only ... easier said than done. *Who really wants magazines anyway?*

The day went on. Laurie and I had Cooking Group. We vowed to NOT cause the firemen to come, even though it had been a delight. As we were starting to prep cooking, Bud, ninety-one, walked into the kitchen. Seeing Harriet, he fondly said, "I know you." We watched them catch up on the past SEVENTY-THREE years! Bud referred to Harriet as, "never getting over it," explaining, "She had a crush on me." I expected a denial, but she only giggled as if she was eighteen versus eighty-nine and said, "I guess I did." Because I was thirty-nine years old, it was fascinating to me that they reviewed that period of life as if it were yesterday. *Some things are not washed away by years. What old boyfriend might I want to see in forty years?*

I made it back into the break room, looking for a snack other than my candy. I was more the salty carb sort. Glancing at the paper, I saw a couple names. *Yay! Tomorrow will bring more.*

Then I wondered, *Where's my Lena today? Haven't seen her ... I will check.* I found her down the hall sitting closely to the aviary, listening to the birds flit and chirp. She could hear them en mass in their screened-in enclosure.

"Hey Lena, how's your day?"

"My Mary," her aged tremulous voice said slowly and sweetly as if singing a lullaby in my ear.

I asked, "Are you enjoying the bird sounds? Not sure what kind they are but they are so small and dear to watch ... sorry, listen to."

"No apologies needed. I wasn't always blind and now I use my third eye to see them."

"Third eye? I have heard the term but don't really know what it means. One of those new age terms that get used loosely." My mind flitted to the magazine I ordered.

"Obviously, I am not seeing with the visual cortex that I used to, but I see intuitively. Maybe I put my past knowledge together with my other senses and see. Maybe I see what something really is, living energy, when before I was only seeing its form."

"I do know about energy, auras, but have to admit the third eye thing has been a hard one to grasp. Maybe I am being too literal with it." Needing to get back to work, I added, "Lena, you always leave me with something to think about. My mind has felt alive in meeting you."

The edges of her lips curled and she slightly lifted her chin. "Ah, a very fine compliment for an old lady, particularly coming from a millennial." The intent usually carried by that term typically would make me cringe. Instead, I felt an endearing softening cross my lips, sensing surprise she knew the term.

Chapter 7

I HAD A THERAPY APPOINTMENT AFTER WORK. TALK THERAPY was right up my alley since I loved the shit out of processing things ad nauseam. This day, I felt differently going in.

Dr. Lewis waited, as usual, for me to start. Finally, I said, "Today was unique. I didn't find myself thinking, 'If I have to remind one older person that they have memory issues, I'll scream!'

With delving eye contact, she inquired, "That's a good thing. Was it a special day?"

"More the past couple of weeks, not special, but different."

"Yes, it's been several weeks since you've made it in. I wasn't sure if that was a good sign or a worrisome sign."

I didn't feel prepared to say too much yet. "I talked to Barbara, that nurse I have complained about representing my nemesis."

"You mean you talked to her about the quality of your interactions?"

"Yes."

"That's quite a leap. What helped you take that step?"

Divulging more, I told her about Lena and the wind cyclone in the woods. I even told her about stepping out of the shower in record time and having a couple nights of good sleep. She looked at me with a small smile and slight nod. I could tell she was thinking but not saying something. I often saw this expression when she asked a question and I provided my own reason for being stuck. I'd been seeing Dr. Lewis for over a year. Her style was to ask more questions, believing I knew most of my own barriers and sources of demons. On this day, the expression likely stemmed from knowing better than I did that my trajectory was changing.

Maybe to celebrate my day, I fixed a hearty salad loaded with decadent croutons and cheese then looked up third eye. I discovered it's actually located between the eyebrows, not the middle of the forehead as I had thought. I learned that the third eye chakra was associated with the pineal gland in charge of regulating other things, such as sleep and wake time. Apparently, it was located close to the optic nerves and sensitive to changes in lighting. There was something about the perception of altered or "mystical" states of consciousness. *Hmmm, but how does one "make it work"?*

I had a few minutes for a walk before heading off to work. It was Monday, and I was working the later shift so I could be there during both lunch and dinner to see my patients with swallowing issues. My body liked this later shift. I had time to work my head into the game. I always had the drive but getting some fresh air early while I had some energy was pleasing to my psyche.

I walked past the sentry, eventually taking a different loop than my norm. When I neared a familiar intersection from a different direction, I saw the cowboy. *I have passed this spot before and have never seen him. He is five feet tall! I think I would have noticed if he'd been there or maybe I was always looking down since this is near the trail intersection?*

Wearing a ten-gallon hat with a wide brim, his dark eyes were narrow slits. He had long legs, covered in fur chaps. A gun was pulled from his side, but in a ready poise, not a threatening one. *Are the tree people always here, or do they just show up for me? It's a phenomenon I find comforting.* After gazing at him awhile, I knew it was time to get ready for work.

I got there a few minutes early to check the magazine order sheet in the lounge. My heart skipped a beat. I saw numerous orders, but it was Barbara's name that made it skip. She'd ordered THREE magazines. *Did she just like candy, does she really have a heart, or was it her way of telling me she thought about our conversation? No matter what, Matt was ON HIS WAY TO THE ZOO! In a limo!* I couldn't wait for him to come by that evening for the order form.

I had to stop myself from driving crazily home so I could give Matt the form. I realized I didn't even know specifically where he lived, so I'd just have to hope it didn't fall off his radar. Some people actually seemed excited about their magazines. *New Age, I am even excited a little bit.*

I watched some news and talked to my sister, just trying to pass the time. Finally, a knock at the door. I practically slid like I was landing on home base to open it.

"Hi Matt, how's it going?"

"Sorry to bother you. It's Monday, and you said I should come by to get the order form."

As I walked away to get it, I heard him say, "Don't worry if it doesn't have many. I didn't get my hopes up."

I handed him the form as I nonchalantly asked, "Do they tell you how many weeks it takes to start getting the magazines?"

Matt's face reminded me of the old cartoon with eyes popping out from the character's sockets on springs. *Boing.*

"I hope you like the zoo. Oh, and the limo ride, fanceeeeee! When is it?"

Staring at the paper and with a little joyous closed mouth exhale, he slowly responded, "Not for another three weeks."

"That'll be a hard wait but definitely something to look forward to. So ... when will we start receiving magazines in our mailboxes?"

"I will ask. Not sure. Didn't expect to get asked that question!" he beamed proudly. Continuing to slightly shake his head in disbelief, he said, "Wait 'til everyone sees this tomorrow! Wait 'til I show Bella, my foster mom." *I am so curious about the why of this situation, but I know I can't ask. I hardly know him and it's none of my business ... even though people might say that doesn't usually stop me.* Sounding as if he thought he was a bother, he quickly said, "Gotta go. I couldn't concentrate on my homework waiting for enough time to pass before coming down here. Got some math problems to do."

"That is kind of funny. I was waiting for you too. Happy to have helped you out. You know where I live, do you mind if I ask you where you live? I know upstairs."

"In 208. My foster mom is Bella. Thanks again, Miss. You surely made my day ... week."

For a moment, I watched him head down the hall and found myself thinking, *It sure is sweet to be looking into the face of a young, excited person who is now looking forward to life.*

Door shut, TV off, I decided to pull up third eye stuff again on the internet. I wanted to know how to stimulate it.

I read, "Take a few deep breaths in and out and as you do this, visualize the purple energy of the amethyst going into your third eye and filling it up with activated energy. Hold the amethyst in place, close your eyes, and look up directly into the Sun. Allow the Sun to warm the crystal and activate it."

That made no sense to me since looking directly into the sun sounded painful, at the least, and dangerous to the retinas. *Where's the disclaimer: Don't try this at home?* Flipping to another site, *Ah this makes more sense.* It said to sun gaze at the first or last rays of the day when it's safe to look at it. Start out with a few seconds and build up. Other sites suggested communing with nature, lying down under the moon, reading out loud, meditating or practicing yoga. *Maybe my very occasional yoga teacher knows what she's talking about.*

I laid down on the bed thinking I'd do the deep breaths and see about visualizing the third eye, even without the tools. It wasn't very late but I fell asleep and very deeply. When I woke, it was to the light of my alarm coming on. *Holy shit, I slept through the night in my clothes! Even my slippers are still on!*

I got coffee or, as Ryan had always said, "I got half and half and added some coffee." *Too bad, Ryan. Now I can do it whatever way I please!* I sat sipping but noticed I was lavishly rubbing my hand over my thigh when I stopped at a raised area. *Another mole, what the fuck?* This one was about an inch in diameter. I swear I'd not noticed it before now. I looked back at the one on my forearm. No new changes. It seemed stable. Peeking back at my leg, I noticed this one was perfectly round with a smooth surface, smooth edges, and lines with round circles. *This is getting just plain weird.*

I put on my khaki pants and my tennies so I could head out for a hike right after work. I'd be ready to roll. Walking into work, I saw on the board that we were getting a new patient in Room 10. *That's Lena's room!* I raced down the hall, but she wasn't there. My heart pounded. *She was ninety-seven! God, don't let it be what I am thinking!*

Barbara was the first person I saw. "What happened to Lena?" Trying to sound cool, I asked if she went home, even though I knew that was highly unlikely anymore.

"She was moved to Wing II." Then she added, "You look relieved. Did you think she'd died or something? She wasn't even on your speech caseload, was she?" *Mom always said I wear my heart on my sleeve.*

Staring at her while I processed my inner relief, I said, "No, she wasn't," but said no more. I walked away, regaining my composure and strength. I was surprised by the intensity of my reaction.

I had to see a couple patients, but I strategically worked my way down to Wing II. It surely wasn't my favorite wing for people to get transferred to. Seems anywhere I work, there's "that" wing that somehow flies with their own protocol more than the others. Lena should charm them all adequately.

I heard her "Yoohooo" as I walked down the hall. I was pleased to see a CNA, passing by, hear Lena's beckoning sound and walk into her room.

I let her be in there for a moment then entered. "Hi, Tracy, I see you have met my new best friend, Lena." Turning my attention to Lena, I said, "Lena, I am happy to see your face, I had a moment of panic when your bed on the rehab wing had another person in it."

"Don't worry dear, I am not quite dead yet."

Tracy laughed and asked with astonishment, "Is that Monty Python speak?"

Lena followed up with, "Always Look on the Bright Side of Life." Then added, "My dear husband loved singing that song when things felt sour."

My job was done here. Lena had managed to say the one thing to hook Tracy. I had cursory familiarity with Monty Python, but Tracy knew every movie, every obscure line. She'd be back in regularly, probably bringing Monty Python DVDs.

I thanked Tracy for being so on top of it and told Lena I'd be back at some point soon, maybe not until tomorrow. I had a question about some research she'd gotten me thinking about. Lena nodded and pointed to the area between her brows. *Is she an intuitive or what?*

My phone rang after lunch. It was Kelly, "Hey you, kept thinking I'd hear from you. When do you want to take that walk back to the lean-to?"

I was thrilled she'd asked. Too often I had to bribe my friends to go for a hike with me.

Enthusiastically, I asked, "How spontaneous are you feeling? I could go after work today. I get out by four. We'd have enough daylight."

"I'll talk to Rhett and call you back in a bit. He may be able to tag along. We had talked about going in strong since we don't know what weirdo we could encounter."

Chapter 8

THE NEW PERSON IN LENA'S BED DID HAVE orders for a speech eval, well, bedside swallow eval, to be exact. A quarter of my day was spent helping people navigate their memory issues, and it seems the other three-quarters were split with true communication issues such as dysarthria and aphasia, and the types of swallowing issues that were brought to light by Geri Logemann in the late eighties but gained real notoriety in the early nineties.

The genuine communication disorders were certainly the core of my passion and training. Helping people regain their communication was really code for returning their personal power to have more control over their lives. It's incredible how we lose power when we don't have our voice. The compassion-filled family begins by making the decisions, eventually forgetting to even ask for an opinion. Then there's always the "talking for" their family member ... my patient. I have to be quick to call it out. When I do, it's obvious that it's only a reflexive attempt to relieve the uncomfortableness they feel with their loved one's difficulty in communicating. Typically, they are projecting their own uncomfortableness out of love. That becomes one of my quests: to facilitate a comfortableness on both sides ... patient and spouse or patient and child.

I'd been doing this long enough that I had learned theoretically about dysphagia, swallowing disorders, in graduate school. I only had a patient or two over the course of some practicums. I'd learned the hard way about diet and food texture restrictions and circumventing a lack of follow-through issues, especially related to inexperienced staff on the weekends. The jobs of CNAs were incredible, and the pay was so much lower than they deserved. Most were such loving and caring people, and the field was made up of a high percentage of women.

What always made my blood boil was thinking about wage discrepancies. CNAs surely do heavy lifting; they work in harsh conditions (ever been in a long-term care wing on a hundred-degree day?), but most of all, they work to help the elderly maintain a semblance of their dignity at the most vulnerable time of their life. Yet, road workers digging ditches or spreading asphalt make more money. Even flaggers holding stop signs for traffic flow earn about the same as a CNA.

My eyebrows arched up and my head jerked in surprise when I saw the meal tray I had requested being hand-delivered by Barbara. About that time, my phone rang. I moved the tray out of reach and excused myself to the hall. "Rhett can't go but we will be FINE on our own. Did you know I have become a concealed weapon carrier?"

"What? Kelly, no, I didn't know! That's crazy, crazy wild. Rhett is turning you into Annie Oakley. Okay then, we are on. What time?"

•••

When Kelly showed up at my door, I immediately demanded to see the gun. She was the first female, actually the first person, I knew to have a concealed weapon permit. It was TV-like exciting to me. I had fired a gun before but was always impressed when women break that traditional male-pattern behavior. I longed for more of that in myself. The gun was not girly looking and would intimidate for sure. In the way she handled it, I was sure she knew what she was doing.

As we walked on the path, Kelly asked if I'd heard the *NPR Radio-Lab Podcast*, "From Tree to Shining Tree." I hadn't.

"It describes the underground network of systems that runs between trees and the reciprocal relationship between trees and other underground microscopic species. One thing that stuck in my head was how one tree will feed another type of tree when it's sick. It's like billions of little communication fibers sending information and assistance."

Processing that, I exclaimed, "Wow, so while we are busy seeing just what's above ground, there is even more happening below. That seems metaphoric for life and the human's view of the physical world, doesn't it? I do remember learning how a downed tree becomes food for other organisms like lichen. This information is even more intriguing."

"Yeah, if humans could just learn to facilitate and aid like other species do," Kelly added.

We were on a designated mission so we passed by Matt, and when we got to Warrior Tree, I asked Kelly if she could discern a face and body on the tree. She couldn't. She gave a "Hmmmmm, I kind of see it" response when I pointed it out to her. I was used to the "What are you smoking?" sort of reactions to my tree faces. It was my special gift that was of no value but great comfort.

"We go this way," I said as I led us off-trail. Approaching the cairn, my last addition remained the most recent. I was secretly hoping a new one would be added to the mystery. We fell into a silence, Kelly taking my lead of anticipation.

My heartbeat was fast; I could feel a pounding. When we got to the opening, I was startled, maybe shocked. I saw eleven-year-old Matt under the lean-to. He was immersed in a book and didn't even hear us coming.

"Hey you." His eyes shot up with a startle. They settled into surprise after recognizing me, but then his eyes shifted to Kelly.

"This is my friend. What are you doing out here?" I asked Matt.

"I come here all the time. Life feels peaceful, and I can forget why I am not living at home."

Turning to Kelly and gesturing to her and Matt, I said, "This is Kelly. Kelly meet Matt. Does your foster mom know you are here?"

"She figures the woods are safer than where I came from."

"These woods do seem particularly safe, don't they? Caring almost."

Kelly nudged my elbow, whispering, "I guess I don't get to use my gun, do I?"

"Please, shh!" I was sensing some disappointment knowing the mystery had such a simple ending. I wasn't hoping for bad drama, but maybe something that would rattle my world a wee bit more.

"So, the cairns, do you know anything about them?" I asked.

Matt replied, "Yeah, someone else added two rocks, so I added another. Looked the same this time. Did you build it?"

"Noooo, but I added the two rocks. How long have you been coming here?"

"I started walking in here soon after moving to Bella's, my foster mom's, about six months ago. But I only found this spot last month. The cairn was here then."

"How do you two know each other?" Kelly interjected.

"Mary helped me sell some magazines for school." He looked at me, grinning, with eyes glinting and hands clasped in a champion mode. His words rushed out, "I get that limo ride and night at the zoo next Friday!" With a laugh of joy, I returned the champion celebration gesture.

Looking and pointing up, I asked. "Any idea who built that?"

"Not really, but I did see a footprint one of the first times here, in some mud when it was wet from the rain. Could have been yours, just know it was too big to be mine."

Raising my eyebrows and piecing information together, I said, "You have been coming here for a month. I have only been here to this lean-to once, about two weeks ago." Feeling a tinge of excitement to know the mystery wasn't completely over, I added, "We have yet another visitor who needs discovering. Someone with some survival skills to build the lean-to and platform. We will probably find our cairn creator too."

Shrugging her shoulders, Kelly said, "Or just an Eagle Scout or experienced camper."

I looked more closely at the lean-to. The way some parts were interwoven, someone definitely had a skill unknown to me. Kelly and I were looking at the rope ladder and trying to figure out how we could get up there. I was able to get my hands up to the third rung, but the rope-swinging aspect made it hard to get any upward momentum. I just kept swinging into the tree. Kelly said it wasn't her thing to try something athletic. Matt popped up. At four-feet-something, he could get his hand on the second rung. Having been on monkey bars more recently than I had, he did a dyno move up to the third rung. He apparently had done this before because he knew to sway into the tree with one foot ready to hook his heel on a notch hidden in the tree. That gave him enough stability to lift his other leg up to a rung. The rest was history. I tried a few times, but couldn't get the same momentum he demonstrated. Not being one to flounder in front of others, I said I'd keep practicing.

"We may as well head out. Want to go with us, Matt, or stay here? I think I'd feel better if you came, but it's up to you."

He joined us, and I asked him, "What book are you reading?"

"*Earth Abides*. It's an apocalypse story but not all gory. There's a disease where just about everyone dies. I know I am supposed to like blood and gore at my age, but I like the power of the earth in this."

"Wow, Matt. That is both unique and refreshing."

We reached the cairn, and I believe we all had a simultaneous thought as we looked from the cairn to each other.

"Great minds think alike!" We each added one stone to the cairn.

Kelly wasn't likely to return, even though she was a teeny bit intrigued by the place. Matt and I agreed that if one of us returned and the cairn was changed, we would report it to the other.

"Matt, I know you come here regularly, but are you sure you feel safe?"

"Sure, I do. I can tell, these are the good woods."

Kelly left when we reached her car. Even though there was still plenty of daylight, I walked Matt up to his apartment. He had a key, but his foster mom must have heard our voices approaching and came out to say hello. Matt introduced me to Bella as the lady downstairs who helped him sell the magazines. She seemed somewhere between grateful and understandably leery, asking what I did for a living.

After a brief explanation, I offered, "Since I work with geriatrics, it was quite inspiring to do something positive for a smiling young face."

I didn't indicate where we ran into Matt since I didn't want her wondering why we were all in the woods. Yet, I questioned if I should now that we know there's another player in this woods story.

Chapter 9

I SAT ON MY PATIO AFTER RETURNING TO MY apartment. The sun was in that getting-ready-to-set phase, so I decided to try the third eye, the staring-at-the-sun thing. Looking at one, non-moving anything for five minutes was much harder to do than I expected. I was glad it was suggested to build up to five minutes, so I didn't feel I was too shallow of a metaphysic.

Over the past few weeks, I had been weaning myself from the Lexapro, even though I knew I probably shouldn't. I seemed to be sleeping and feeling better. I would give my doctor a heads up.

I was in the woods; my eyes were closed, but I was seeing a gleam like dew and those sparks floating between trees that looked like the ones I had noticed after the wind cyclone. I was sensing a peaceful joy and tingling of my skin, particularly on my forearm.

I woke up from this dream and wrote it down. Applying Jeremy Taylor's thinking, I was struck that there were no other characters, so I couldn't consider what characteristics of a person were attempting to communicate awareness to me.

I suppose there are the trees. What do I have in common or what do I think of trees? Trees are comforting to me. They are appreciated by some but ignored by most unless they want to "use them." They have a hidden strength that allows for survival. I'm not sure they are given a choice, but they help even the takers.

●●●

I got in the shower. I felt like lingering there luxuriously, feeling the steam encompass me, the singe of the pelting. Noticeably, my lingering didn't come from the usual dread of the world and work, but more from pondering. *That dream sounds a hell of a lot like me!* I tried to think back to the sparks and glistening. *I'd love to feel a spark, a glistening.*

I had to rush since I lingered longer in the pondering than I tended to when filled with the dread. I walked into work with a sense of anticipation.

"You going to eat lunch with us today or spend it with patients?" Laurie asked.

Being an OT, she, too, spent much of her typical lunch hour helping patients. Her career quest was helping patients regain hand-to-mouth skills for eating or figuring out strategies or devices that could improve their independence. Over time, our lunch "hour" had shrunk to lunch half hour, sometimes spent documenting, and always coming well after traditional lunch. Patients were often napping after being worn out by the regimen of rehab schedule. Few people realize how far an octogenarian can slip physically in a mere few days of hospitalization. Nor do they realize how much energy is used for tracking every swallow consciously or learning to eat with a non-dominant hand due to the other being paralyzed from a stroke.

"I am going to eat while I chat with Lena today, but tomorrow we have a date! I promise."

Lena was up in a chair by her window. The spring breeze gently caused the curtain to tap against the heater. I asked if she could hear it and if it was bugging her, but she apparently liked the rhythm of the auditory feedback since she didn't have the visual.

"The breeze is wonderful, almost balmy."

I explained, "First flowers are starting to come up in the courtyard. Spring is around the corner."

Sniffing as if she could smell them, she said, "I love the first narcissus. Tulips are when you know spring is here."

"Hey Lena, you mentioned the third eye the other day. I looked it up and found out it's been a thing since Ancient Egyptian times. It sits near the pineal gland. It's part of the endocrine system like the thyroid. I found some exercises for activating it, and sat on my deck staring at the setting sun, but it only made me sleepy and I couldn't focus for five minutes, the time recommended. Are you really able to activate it? Can you really "see" with it? Is it a sense? How do you know it's open?"

"That's a lot of questions," she softly chuckled. "Yes, sort of, yes. I can tell you what I feel when mine is open. I feel warmth and a sense of pressure in between my eyes. Pleasing pressure; not headache pressure. It may be better described by pushing out pressure, inside out, versus pushing in, if that makes sense."

"Do you recall how long it took you to get it to work?"

"Seems at first, it'd flit open and shut quickly. I don't recall anymore. Months maybe. I would think it has to do with the type of attempts, frequency, all that." Furrowing her brows and shifting her head toward me, she asked, "What are you eating? I hear you crunching."

"Kohlrabi," I responded with an exaggerated crunch.

"Ah, I used to love that. My teeth won't let me have it anymore. Did you grow it?"

"No, no garden in my apartment. But with spring approaching, it is starting to show up in stores. There's always plentiful amounts because most people don't know what it is."

I finished the last bite and said I had to get back to work. I could tell she liked the company, but Lena never made any, even subtle, gestures toward letting me know she'd love me to stay.

Instead, I asked her, "Do you have family, Lena, anyone who comes and takes you out or lingers for a long time?"

"If you live to be ninety-seven, you have the sad opportunity of seeing most of your people pass over. No, pretty much just me and a distant cousin who lives a thousand miles away."

"See ya soon, Lena. Let's at least enjoy the courtyard together when it's warmer." As I was heading to the door, she said, "Oh another thing I remember about my third eye—sometimes I saw lights, sparks, but not very often."

I was thinking, *how uncanny*, but I only said, "Keep thinking. Would love more of your beta."

"My what?"

"Your firsthand knowledge. Your guidance." Walking down the hall, I thought of the sparks after the windstorm.

Chapter 10

I HAD TO RE-EVALUATE MR. TALBOT'S TOLERANCE FOR GROUND food. He had returned a few hours prior from his video fluoroscopy, the test to determine how his swallow muscles were functioning, and it indicated no liquid was seeping into his airway. No aspiration. Maybe it was some spontaneous healing of the musculature; I prefer and do believe his willingness to comply with the exercises was the answer.

Either way, it was great news because he wanted to be able to eat his wife's canned fruits and vegetables next winter. *I absolutely love he just assumes he will still be in this world. Guess we never stop looking to the future.*

"I know, Mr. Talbot, you'd rather just jump to steak and potatoes, but we can move through these diet changes now at a much faster pace since we know there's no generalized aspiration. I get that you are so over pureed foods." Flicking my hand in a magic wand motion while removing the lid from the food I'd carried in, I said, "Puree diet be gone!" as I revealed the small cubes of carrots and the shredded pieces of chicken with gravy.

He beamed. His Paul Newman blue eyes twinkled. I can only assume this would be like me being without popcorn for weeks on end. So much has changed about Mr. Talbot since he arrived four weeks ago. Self-feeding had eased. He was physically stronger. These were the successes that keep rehab workers going.

Like a hawk, I watched all aspects of the oral phase as he took a few bites. I had him start with the carrots since they held more moisture. I watched the size of bite he took, lip closure on the spoon, signs of moving the bolus of food from front to back, how long it took to swallow. Following every bite, I asked him to vocalize to listen to his voice. Yay, all clear, no clinging residue in the pharynx or throat. Next came the chicken with some gravy. Same observation, same check, yay. All three bites clear. Final test, the chicken without gravy. It wasn't dry, it just wouldn't be as easy to hold together in the mouth and required a stronger swallow. As I watched him, the remnants of his youth helped me see what a tall, wide-shouldered farmer he had been. Such a catch he had to have been.

"That went down okay, but it was a little more work. Can I get gravy on all my meat?"

"Yes, sir. That will be part of the order. For now, if it doesn't get served that way, please ask. The muscles may tire a bit since you have had just puree for several weeks. As you eat this diet, the muscles will continue to improve and coordinate better. Soon we can try that steak; not tomorrow though," I said as I pointed a cautionary finger at him.

"Understood, boss lady. Ask for gravy if it doesn't show up that way ... check."

With a sadder tone, I added, "The downer, can't start until tomorrow. I really need to be in the building. I have learned to respect these steps up the 'food chain,'" I said with quote fingers. Using my brightest smile, I continued, "It will start with real pancakes or eggs in the morning though!"

With his blue eyes squinted, he said, "You are a cold-hearted one. Tease me with this and give me blended peas for dinner." He took back the rest of the chicken with gravy and the carrots. "If puree is for dinner, I may as well eat all of this now," he added with a smirk.

I observed the rest, and smiling, I left the room with a, "Always a delight, you are. I will be sad when you fly the coop to your farm. See ya in the morning."

A couple glitches in billing got me out into traffic later than expected. On the highway, someone was trying to cut in front of me to avoid slowing down for the truck that they didn't plan ahead to move around. *You had a half-mile opportunity to see this coming, but no, you have to wait, and you want over now.* Instead of speeding up or pretending I didn't see him, I just smiled and gestured to slide in. *I have noticed surprise cognitive glimpses into my thought patterns. It wasn't like me to be so generous. Surly better describes my usual driving persona. Now, if only I could shift that at work.*

Chapter 11

I GOT HOME, PETTED TEQUILA FOR A WHILE, AND took off for the woods. I wanted to check out my cowboy tree a little closer. *What should I name him? Festus, Slim? I will think about that.* I had been sure to grab the amethyst rock. I had kept it mostly because I loved purple and this was a lovely shade. I wanted to believe in the power of the energy from rocks or crystals but couldn't say that I did.

Hurrying past Matt, I waved and made a quick connection: *This sweet bouffant-haired tree had the same name as upstairs Matt. Hmm.* I had to remember exactly where I veered off after seeing Warrior Tree. It wasn't in my usual stretches. Not sure why I wanted to see this one again. Maybe because its distinct body and posture seemed unique for my trees; they were typically just heads. I wanted to see if it was still that way or if I had imagined it. Most people thought I imagined or exaggerated them anyway. Especially because I swore that one day they weren't there and the next they were. "Uh-huh, sure," was the standard response. He was there! *Yes! I am not crazy!* I'd brought a little mat to sit on. I loved the woods but not the dirt that much. I sat down, tried to get comfortable, gazed at Cowboy for a while, and recalled my amethyst. I pulled it from my possibility pouch and rolled it around in my hand. Feeling a little silly, I placed it at my so-called third eye.

I sat that way for what seemed like fifteen minutes, but when I checked my watch, it was only two minutes. My arm was tiring, so I put it down on the ground. It was its original birthplace anyway. I closed my eyes and listened to the birds. There must have been a large number of them in a tree behind me. I listened to the fluttering among branches and the group chirping, some sounding more insistent than others, as if it were a lively meeting about who would nest where. *Wonder what kind they are. I am only sure of a robin's sound.*

I always sucked at meditation. My mind was very hard to quiet. Maybe it was the "Idle hands are the devil's workshop" plaque that hung on our kitchen bulletin board for the entire fourteen years I lived in my childhood house. It was never referred to, but even my sister recalls it. *Mary, ignore that tickle, it's nothing. Breathe, keep listening.* I couldn't help it. I swept my hand over it. The tickle was at the mole on my thigh. *Get it back, refocus.*

I bolted upright and gasped at the same time. My eyes flung open and I looked around. Could have sworn I heard, "Hello, glad you came back." I saw no one. Leaning every which way, I looked at trees from a different angle to check behind them. No one. *I am sure I heard someone's voice. Wonder if it was whoever built that tree stand and lean-to?*

"Hello?" Nothing. "Hello, hello?" in my friendliest, most confident voice. Silence. Even the birds were silent.

A bit on edge, I tried but I couldn't really settle in again; I decided to just head home. I didn't feel afraid, but yet my brain was asking, *Is it a good idea to meet that person? I have no clue if it is a male or female, a sage or pervert, a homeless person, survivalist, or merely an adventurist. Should I leave something at the cairn to suggest a meet and greet? What if Matt found that person first and it didn't go well. I would feel responsible. Should I tell his foster mom he shouldn't go there for a while?*

Caution had controlled so much of my life. Overthinking before I acted. Opportunities missed by delays. Not believing I could achieve or just deciding to play it safe. Years ago, I thought I'd be great as a speech-language pathologist in a private practice, but I was afraid to go without the known paycheck. I also realized I had a big problem with "going big." Not just believing I could succeed but questioning who I was to "go big," BE "big in a room," to outshine. Bringing others to the forefront became my modus operandi. Believing in others took up my time, so I didn't have to ask, "Why don't I do that?"

As I walked, I found myself continuing to self-flagellate for all my fear-based life choices. My most catastrophic thought pattern was the one about being sued, found guilty of something, and going to prison, forced to live the *Orange Is the New Black* life. That was my middle-of-the-night rumination.

Deep in thought, I was back at the complex without seeing anything along the way. I even forgot to say bye to Bouffant Matt.

"Hi, how's it going?" Appearing behind me as I was opening the door to the complex was Matt's foster mom. We were heading the same way. We looked to be the same age, but she was taller, probably five feet nine-ish, and was what they used to call "big boned," bringing along an air of confidence in her stature.

"Good lately. Work is swamped and that's okay until they make you feel you can't be sick or take time off." I stopped as I heard myself start out positive and slide right to the negative. "How are you?"

She answered, "Good. When I decided to foster care, I became my own manager. That was a welcomed change."

I decided to bring up the woods. "I wasn't sure if I should mention it, but the day I came back with Matt, my friend and I had run into him in the woods. He's a confident young man, but I am wondering if there's someone else hanging out in the woods. I saw a lean-to and a tree loft. Today I could have sworn I heard someone tell me hi, but I didn't see signs of anyone."

Following a short pause, almost weighing her words, she said, "Oh, that lean-to has been there for some time. Don't think you need to worry about it. Matt loves those woods and I remember how much time I spent in them when I was a kid. I lived down the street. It's always been a pretty safe area."

"Well, that is reassuring. Matt sure seemed comfortable in them. The hello thing could have been my imagination. I just knew I'd feel better if I mentioned it."

She headed upstairs, and I went down the hall to my apartment. I was praising myself for telling about seeing Matt, not keeping quiet. *No jail time in that story ending. Geesh, I look so self-assured to outsiders.*

Walking into the apartment, I was warmed by the eastern late afternoon sun coming in. I changed into my shorts and a T-shirt. I still liked my shirt that said, "Still she persisted" and all the other character traits of the strong women who spoke without being intimidated by anyone.

Tequila took no time pouncing up on the table, waiting to lick the oil that would remain once I finished with my salad. Slowly she leaned one leg down off the table edge and was rubbing her paw over my new-ish leg mole. Cats were always graceful, but this was unusually gentle. She seemed, as strange as it sounds, comforted. As she stroked it, she purred. *Hmmm, do I follow general medical advice and get these two spots checked out, or do I follow Tequila's animal instinct that all is well?*

The breeze coming in the open patio door was incredibly soothing. I sat and listened as it worked its way through the series of apartment buildings. As I scanned the room from my chair, I realized I had come to love my place. I had gradually replaced the things that belonged to "us" with items that pleased me to sit on, be around, and hold in my hand. Although I had released some of the anger from the divorce, those "us" items often served to remind me that I was the chameleon, and when I wasn't just blending, I was acquiescing to keep the clunking gears from stopping altogether.

I left my plate for Tequila, who quickly took to lapping. One of my favorite sounds was listening to the delicate lapping of her tongue. I took my tea to the futon and started Googling more about the third eye. *I used to love this shit. I went underground with so much of it because of silences or snarky remarks. It was easier than trying to defend my position with a master quick thinker who started most arguments with the intention to win and persuade versus learn or communicate.*

I read, "May feel a sense of pressure between the eyebrows." It went on to describe an increase in intuition and changes in life perspectives, along with more self-reliance. It also referenced circular shapes and lights.

Hmmm. Closest I am thinking I get to any of this is having seen some lights... those sparks, not the same as the lights I think this means ... but maybe. I have always wanted to be "gifted" in something. Always felt so ordinary, not bland, but close.

Chapter 12

A S THE SHOWER WAS RAINING OVER MY BODY, I listened to a podcast. Not my usual shower routine, but someone recommended it. It was perfect for the shower. A guru of some kind was talking about the dramatic shift in thinking and vision that stems from taking cold showers. He suggested starting by standing under the water while the water was heating up. *Not sure I ever care enough about spiritual development for that!* My preference is to turn the water on to full hot, let the steam build a bit, and then step in. Even a second of cold water is torturous.

The drive to work was mindless. I knew a number of patient discharges were pending, so the census would be decreasing. Saner days were just around the corner. I checked in on Mr. Talbot since he was getting scrambled eggs and hash browns.

"Woohoo!" I said when he raised a bite of potatoes in a "toast" to the new diet.

All was well on that front, I said after a few minutes of observation, and asked Cindy, the CNA, to let me know if she heard any coughing or a gurgly voice as he continued.

I needed to see George next. He was eating in his room. Since the vast majority of patients were eighty-plus, George seemed like a live wire to only be in his sixties. Per his history, he'd been abusing alcohol, and even though he was engaging, it was in a curmudgeon manner. He surely didn't like being told how to eat and when to get up, and he definitely didn't like being expected to exercise. We all used our best cajoling skills to gain compliance. He was never going to enjoy the rehab process, just endure it. He wasn't holding much hope of getting back home, where his wife had already been a primary caregiver anyway. The right-sided paralysis was going to challenge her ability to manage him.

As soon as I walked in, alarms sprang out of my head. I lurched toward his tray, because I could see his milk was regular, not the thickened consistency he needed and was ordered. He hated the thickened liquids, but he aspirated on thin liquids. As I lurched, he snatched up his glass.

"You're not taking this," he said. As he spoke, his voice sounded wet like he needed to clear his throat. There was a spontaneous cough, and luckily it cleared.

"George, you can't drink more of that! It's not safe. It's going to end up in your lungs!" As I spoke, I could see a couple sips had already been taken. The kitchen sent the wrong drink, and the server didn't notice.

"You're not taking it away. I am sick of the other stuff. It doesn't taste like milk."

"Don't drink it! You know you need it thickened. It's not a game. You could end up with pneumonia!" While glaring at me, he took a sip, more like a gulp. It went beyond the gurgled voice quality to one that sounded like he was physically underwater.

"Cough, George, cough."

I left the room; Barbara was right outside passing out medications. Counting.

"Barbara, you need to check George. You need to check George's lungs."

Leaving the cart meant putting away what she'd started and locking it. Not a preference during rounds. Rounds were a sacred time.

"I can't come right now; I'll be there as soon as I pass this."

I started to walk away. Got about two feet, swung around, and said slowly, firmly, "No, you. need. to. come. now. He's aspirated. He needs you STAT, NOW."

Other heads turned. Our eyes met for a moment of surprise. Both surprised by my tone and both surprised that she hurried into the room.

Mandy, another nurse, was right behind her. Within moments, they whipped the curtain closed around him and were preparing to suction, even though he was protesting in a full-blown gurgled tone. I left the room and went into the documentation room. About five minutes later, I heard an ambulance. As they wheeled him from the room, his eyes met mine. Where I expected to see fear or thankfulness, there was anger. I wondered if I had spoiled plans beyond just drinking thin liquids.

I went to the staff one-sitter restroom. Locked the door. I stared in the mirror. My knees felt rubbery, so I sat on the toilet, head in my hands, covering my eyes. That was the first time I had heard someone sound as if they were talking while underwater. I didn't know how George was going to be. If I was honest with myself, my overriding thoughts were about feeling more stunned by my demanding behavior with Barbara and its result. *Shit, where did that come from? I always hoped in a crisis I'd step up. Recalling traveling in Michigan and witnessing two cars collide on ice; helping the bloody-faced woman to the curb and calming her. I had always felt like the young woman who responded that day was left there some fifteen years earlier.* A slight smile came over my face. *She's baaack.*

Someone knocked on the door. Everyone preferred the private restroom to the three-staller, just for a few moments away from the ding of the room lights, the voices, the hiss of the oxygen machines. This place was a momentary respite from obligations, tugs in multiple directions that on a bad day left you feeling drawn and quartered.

I opened the door and walked out feeling lighter, as if something had been removed. I saw Barbara as I returned to the floor, immersed in continuing her med pass. Touching her elbow, I said, "Thanks, Barbara, for being so quick with knowing what to do. It probably saved his life."

"Hopefully it did, not so sure. I will let you know what I hear." I started to walk away when she called, "Mary." Turning back to her, I heard, "You did well too. He is not one to be told what to do."

I wondered if I looked as proud as I was feeling inside. I knew a compliment from Barbara shouldn't have such an impact. Really, who was she to determine how I felt? It had more to do with making a decision, forcing it through, followed by an acknowledgment from someone from whom I knew it didn't come easy.

I asked Laurie to meet me for a drink after work; I had something I wanted to celebrate. When we arrived at 3 Amigos, I said, "Margaritas are on me!"

Laurie leaned in, whispering, "Hey I heard about George today. He sure could be stubborn. I heard you got nursing there ASAP and probably kept him from dying. Is that what we are celebrating?"

"Partially. You know my angst with Barbara and how I feel she consciously opposes so many of my requests? ... The real celebration is I got a compliment from her today."

"No shit! What did she say?"

"She went out of her way to tell me I had done well today. I was walking away from her and she actually stopped me and told me I had done well. In front of people, no less!"

"You are moving up, girl! I did hear from Mandy you pretty much made her jump! That had to be difficult I bet."

"Surprisingly, it wasn't. I have no idea where it came from. It felt like my only choice. It welled up from the deep and had to be spoken."

The margs arrived. Being a parent of a fifth-grader, Laurie said, "A toast! A toast to Mary's growing and changing!"

Even though Laurie had to scoot after one drink, it had been great to boast to someone who completely shared the moment with me.

Lying on my bed, I listened to the podcast *From Tree to Shining Tree* again. It was fascinating. It was my third time through after Kelly told me about it. It was engaging but packed with new ideas. I always longed to be that person who could remember new information with one run-through. It took me longer to integrate. Even after hearing it, I needed time to organize it in my head so I could actually talk intelligently about it.

More and more, I had been keeping my amethyst with me. I'd stored it in a two-by-three pouch I'd gotten years ago. My friend had called it a possibles pouch. I loved little pouches but had no teeny treasures. This amethyst felt a bit guardian-like. I placed it at my third eye as I listened. I wasn't sure what I hoped or expected to happen. Just opening up to whatever it could be.

There was so much about the forest communication system that was absolutely intriguing. I was now forming a clear picture of the interwoven and purposeful activity beneath my feet.

So, trees not only communicate with each other and across species, they both warn and help each other. We see the tip of the iceberg. The stoic persona, the physical beauty, but too often we forget how alive the trees are. I suppose we do that so we can use their wood for our construction purposes and feel okay about it.

I dozed as I was listening. I immediately slipped into a world in which I was standing on a grassy knoll, but beneath the ground. I could see fibers stretching for miles running from one tree to the next. Everything entwined, working in cooperation to nourish. When I woke, the sun was setting. I decided to go out on my patio and watch the setting sun. I passed Tequila, who was basking in the last rays. Her face was eyes-down, snuggled between her paws to receive the warmth but not the brightness. Beyond adorable.

I have been using this amethyst and looking at the setting sun thing for a week. Let's see what comes of it. I'd say morning sun, that ain't going to happen. I am waking up better than I was for months, but I'm not that zealous yet.

It was almost at the horizon. It didn't hurt my eyes to gaze. I set the timer on my phone. *I think I made it one or two minutes before. I will aim for five.* I gazed and found I attended to it longer. My mind wandered to the woods, momentarily to my tree faces, but I kept gazing. *Why are they mostly males? Why do I see them so readily while others do not? What does it mean, or even matter, that I see them anyway? What's Matt upstairs doing right now? Is Barbara as astonished as I am with my tone and that she did what I asked?* Yoo-hoo. The timer told me five minutes were done. *Five minutes, I do feel relaxed. That's something for me.*

Chapter 13

I WOKE UP DECIDING TO SQUEEZE IN A QUICK bike ride on the trainer. I went right to my favorite songs. *Uprising* by Muse. It always made me bike fast, and I belted out the words. Suddenly, I realized they included the words "third eye." *Third eye! Never paid attention to that before! It's always been the words, but suddenly I hear them.*

Then came Katy Perry's *Firework*. I knew these were old, but I was taken away by them, and the energy spun my wheels for me. Her words were blaring through my headphones, my arms were rhythmically pounding the air to the beat. My upper body raised up and down, forward and back.

The next song was *Believe It* by Cimorelli. I heard the words a bit differently this time. My self-believe had been nudged.

I was fully into the flow of my bike ride when *Brave* by Sara Bareilles came on. I had spoken up and it had made a difference to me.

I have no idea how many times my mind has replayed that moment with Barbara. That's good rumination, right? At least it wasn't my usual berating of myself or saying over and over, "I should have said ..." This had to be better, praising myself, patting myself on the back. I haven't done this in a long time. I should thank those ladies for the encouragement.

I think I floated into work. I felt joy knowing I hadn't dragged, trudged, or felt some level of dread every single day. *Grab it while I can. I'm sure the old me will return all too soon. She feels in charge when she does wake. Sometimes I feel the "happy me" can only step aside and let depressed me get it out of her system. "Choose to be happy." That's bullshit. I feel controlled or zombified by "sad me." Maybe I should give her her own name. I don't want to keep feeling that she is "me."*

My face flattened and my psyche fleetingly panicked as I acknowledged three eval orders on my desk. *Now that's a buzzkill. It's as if my shadow side went on the hunt just to dampen my rising spirit. Stop it happy Mary, get on with it. Got woods to visit after work.* I checked in with the schedule board to arrange my day. The OTs got in so early since they had to work on self-dressing and bathing skills. They got the pick of the early hours. But then I surely didn't want to have to be there by 7:00 a.m. It's the PTs I usually had more trouble working around.

I love my PT friends, but most Physical Therapists do get placed at the top of the pecking order in rehab importance. Patients don't help my situation. All too often, they see the PT as right up there with the doctor. I suppose it is because PT has so much more notoriety across the "health care board." I can admit it, some envy at play. I'd love to have the public just know what an SLP does. No explaining myself. Moving on, I can hope these evaluations are the classic stroke.

I loved nothing better than helping that classic aphasia patient. It brought joy to see them regain the ability to express their ideas, understand what people were saying, say that word they really meant, and not the word that for some godforsaken reason popped out in its place.

I got my schedule set, and knew it was best to get the evals done as quickly as possible. *With my current caseload and now the evals, I hope I can find time to see Lena. I want to update her on my third eye quest. Not that I have anything to report, more that I am trying. Not many others I can share this with. In fact, no one.*

I looked at the history of my first eval, Hazel. She sounded quite impacted. I was hopeful for much spontaneous recovery as I walked in to see a bright-eyed woman, looking hopeful herself. I introduced myself. She nodded. I explained who I was, what I'd be doing. I used as many gestures and visuals as I could until I knew how my words were landing. I could immediately see she was using the "aphasia nod" and not processing what I was saying. But then, speech pathology can be a language of its own with terms such as "receptive language," which is a fancy way to say "understand." That's just the easy level of professional lingo.

Remembering my own ahas from the book *My Stroke of Insight* by Jill Taylor, a scientist who had a massive brain hemorrhage in her thirties, I consciously slowed my speaking rate, quieted my voice, and placed what felt like oddly uncomfortable pauses between requests and comments. I simplified my word choice. I tended to have a booming voice and, according to that author, noise stimulated a nails-on-the-chalkboard response. I was sure that's not universal, but it was worth being aware of.

I pulled out photos from the Western Aphasia Battery and began asking her to point to pictures I was saying. In a set of two, only 30 percent. *Crap.* I tried letters of the alphabet, and got no better results. Her face became flatter, knowing she didn't know.

I saw a photo album on her dresser, and picked it up. Someone had wisely taped names under each of the photos. *Thank God for that.* I asked her to show me Bill—correct! I continued with a high rate of success. I didn't know at the time if she knew my word or read the name she'd probably written for decades. I was just thrilled she was successful. Her persona relaxed too. Even though I thought I had become pretty damn good at hiding my, "Ah shit, wrong again" face and body language, they always knew. *Yay! A starting point and something positive to tell her family.* Having something purposeful that the family could spend time doing helped lift everyone's spirits. Lending hope was a key.

I recognized Hazel had been very quiet, so with having had some success, I shifted to the next area of checking her expression. I asked her to repeat some words, but she only opened her mouth. No sound came out. I asked her to imitate some mouth movements, and she did. I asked her to imitate some hand movements, and she did. I demonstrated pushing down to achieve a grunt and motioned for her to push against my hand in the same fashion. There was a faint sound with that. Aphonia wasn't typical with a stroke, but the vocal folds or innervation of the nerves could be impacted. I tried exclamations in unison, "Oh no!" and "uh-uh." I saw facial expressions commensurate with the message. But no sound. Finally, I tried singing, "Happy birthday to you, Happy birthday." Ah! A bit of hummed sound. Voice.

"Mrs. Smith, thank you so much for your time. We will do this every day. We have some good things to start with." I made sure everything she needed was within reach before I left: water, call light, phone. *I will need to see what she can do with her phone tomorrow. Maybe a hello?* I smiled, waved goodbye, and she waved back. *God, I hope for substantial spontaneous recovery.*

I saw Laurie further down the hall, and asked her how Mrs. Smith had done following directions during her eval. She said, "She seems to have some agnosia, difficulty knowing how to use functional dressing items, but she did manage to dress herself with demonstration. She followed very predictable routines, but I'm not sure she was really understanding my words."

I recommended, "Please give her lots of visuals and intonations to help with processing. Speak slower, not louder, just slower with frequent pauses to give her brain time to catch up. It's hard to know at this stage which things are or are not getting through, and which ones just need added time. Maybe I will try to observe a bit tomorrow morning. Thanks, friend."

Chapter 14

IT WAS AN AMAZING EARLY SPRING AFTERNOON, AND I wanted nothing more than to grab an apple and head back to the woods. I packed the apple, my small mat, some water, the amethyst possibility pouch, and a PB sandwich that I decided to make at the last minute. Not sure why, just had the urge.

I didn't know if I was brave or stupid for being so curious about the other person in the woods. *Was I brave to confront it, or stupid to pursue danger?* It felt like one of those horror movies where everyone in the audience is saying, "No! Don't do it!" or "That's ridiculous, who would go back in there, really?!"

When I thought back, the voice was friendly, not ominous. But was that because a trap was being set, or was it because the person WAS friendly. Maybe they were just being careful themselves for some reason. *Ugh, it really sucks to be a person who can argue every angle. I guess I do have a gift. However, I seem to use the skill when it's likely to cause me the most angst, not when I am trying to make my case to someone in a friendly debate.*

I stopped and waved to Bouffant Matt, apologized for racing by the other day, but hoped he understood. Got to Warrior Man and realized I hadn't decided if I would go right toward the cairn or ahead toward

Cowboy. I decided to head to Cowboy. There was enough daylight, I could probably do both if I felt so inclined. I wanted to prove to myself I would still see and hear the persona I thought I had noticed last time.

He was still there. Gun just out of his holster, fur-lined chaps and all. "Howdy Partner." I stood there, head cocked to the side, checking out his details from close up. He was an aspen and the deer had nibbled or there'd been weather-wearing, but whatever it was, it had formed him completely. Less apparent close up but unmistakable from a distance ... to me.

I settled on my mat, my back supported by another tree. I looked at the strong aspen. I'd read they grow in groups and if one dies, the "family" dies out too. Although anything you read these days, you can find ten things to contradict any single piece of information. That's just like the arguments in my head. The internet or AI has its own mental health struggles.

Pulling out my amethyst, I gazed at it. I rolled it around in my hand, noticing it had a rounded point and six sides to the top. It really looked like it was designed to be a necklace. I didn't know what they looked like coming out of the ground, but I doubted they emerged this clean.

I crossed my legs, attempted to take a yoga "om" pose with one hand open on my knee, while holding my amethyst to my third eye with the other. I was feeling like I was doing a great job clearing my mind when I heard a rubbing sound ahead in the woods. Strangely not feeling panic, I opened my eyes to see a deer rubbing its hind quarters on a tree, probably trying to rid some of the winter fur. He seemed unaware or uncaring of me. I closed my eyes after watching him do this for a couple minutes. I settled in, trying to see the deer in my mind. I saw some of the patches where the wintery gray coat had shed, giving way to a rich, soft brown. *Amazing how the animal kingdom is protected by their changing colors to match the fauna of their own surroundings.* In my mind, I watched myself gracefully move up to the deer and stroke the soft but wiry fur.

As in yoga balance poses, I tried to focus on one spot on the deer to hold my attention still. My arm was getting tired again. I moved the stone to my leg and felt a warmth where it'd been. *Probably the warm air contacting the spot that had been covered. "Focus, Mary."*

"Hello, again. Don't be startled. You're safe here."

Leaping to my feet, I looked around. This time, I definitely heard the voice coming from in front of me. The deer had laid in the sun that was filtering through the trees to the forest floor. Its ears were alert but its eyes were closed. *Obviously, it wasn't the deer. There had to be someone.* I didn't recognize the voice as male, female, child, or adult. Knowing too much about voice anatomy, I couldn't fathom how that was possible.

I didn't have the same level of alarm as last time, but I couldn't figure out why someone would talk to me, not once, but twice, and not show themself.

Frustrated, I left. I had no idea where the gumption came from, but when I got to Warrior Man, I bounded off toward the cairn. Of course, there was another stone, but most people add stones to cairns as a version of "I was here."

When I got there, I saw Matt laying under the lean-to. It looked like he was getting to the end of *Earth Abides.*

"This spot makes me feel there could be very few people left on earth," I said.

He looked up casually. This kid didn't startle easily. It made me wonder what he'd been through that an unexpected voice in the woods wasn't alarming him.

He nodded, "I wish I could pick the people who get to remain."

"Who would you pick?"

"Well, I would pick people who are nice to animals, to flowers, and trees. I wouldn't pick mean people."

"Who do you consider to be mean?"

"Bullies for sure. The kids who make fun of me or others because of what we wear or don't have for lunch." I found myself thinking, *Hmmm. He makes a great point. We can all be judged by the way we "wear" what we have been through.*

I smiled gently, "I think I'd like to live in your world that remains. Count me in."

I hadn't told Matt about hearing a voice. I didn't want to alarm him or alter the feeling of respite he found in these woods. Bella seemed to be sure about them, and his safety is her goal. I decided to hang around a bit, and I approached the tree rope to the platform area in the notch of the tree. I flailed into the trunk a few times while Matt watched, and no doubt feeling some pity for the "elder," he asked, "Want me to talk you through it one more time?"

With a small, defeated sigh, I nodded, "Please, but maybe demo. I learn better by watching."

He stretched out to the first rung of the ladder, swinging his legs in toward the tree to build momentum. When he hit the ankle hook notch with his right foot, he was stable and able to reach his right hand up to the second rung. He high-stepped to the first rung with his left foot and simultaneously released his right foot and left hand so both hands were on the second rung, and both feet on the first. He leap-frogged to a standing position, climbing quickly to the platform. He downclimbed with ease, dropping like a spring to the ground.

"Your turn," he said, as he held the bottom of the ladder toward me.

I cocked my head with a questioning look, but then, with my hands on the second rung, I swayed several times toward the tree, contacting the foothold but missing the hook. Matt went over and stretched to mark it with his finger, hoping to make it more apparent. It worked. My heel was hooked, I could move both hands up to the second rung, and it gave me enough space to raise my other foot to the first rung. It was easy to unhook and bring that foot to the rung. Following his leapfrog move, I, too, was soon at the top. As I clung to the platform notch, I gazed around. It was an entirely different view from twenty feet above the usual eye scan. I could see I still had more to explore in these woods. No way to control the rope sway, I took much more time downclimbing, but I made it. "That was fun! Thanks for the beta. It made all the difference."

With a slight proud smile, he said, "I love being helpful. Glad I could."

Chapter 15

WORK HAD EXPLODED AGAIN, WHICH WAS GOOD FOR job security, good for patients who needed the services, but bad timing for where my head was preferring to be. For fourteen days, all I'd had time for after work was stepping in the woods to say hi to Tree Matt, and sitting down to practice meditating for ten or fifteen minutes. No more voices.

By the time I got back to Cowboy, I had my system down pat. Mat, stone, seating position. I more easily slipped into silence and stillness. *Damn the "idle hands, devil's workshop" mantra. Such bullshit we carry.*

I moved the stone away and placed it on my arm where the mole was. I enjoyed the warmth of the pressure that remained between my eyes and felt a pulse from the mole. It was kind of the feel you get from an involuntary muscle twitch but not annoying, more heartbeat-ish.

I heard a soft, definitely fatherly voice say, "I want to speak, but I need you to stay this time."

I subdued a little gasp. I spoke out loud but had a sense it wasn't necessary. "Who are you? Why do you move away, hide?"

"I don't."

"I don't see you when I open my eyes, even when I have looked around. Where do you go?"

"Nowhere."

"Come on. This is a bit maddening. Let me inform you I suck at brain teasers and I am annoyed by most riddles."

"You have been seeing me all along. You just didn't know what you were seeing."

As I opened my eyes, I said, "K, a wee more transparency is needed, please."

A breeze sauntered through, and on it were sparks, but more like fireflies this time.

"Keep your eyes open. Look straight ahead. Why do you think you have chosen this spot, Mary? What do you see?"

Shit, it knows my name! My scan quickly landed on Cowboy.

"Hello, Mary."

Cowboy was illuminated by the fireflies outlining portions of the form I saw as his hat.

"What the fuck. I must be imagining, hallucinating, or going batshit crazy."

"Don't dismiss yourself so easily. I am glad you have kept returning, even though you had no idea why." Nothing resembling a mouth was moving.

I don't think it's talking physically?

"No, you're right, I am not using a body to talk to you." *Shit, I was only thinking that!*

"You don't have to speak for me to hear you."

Well then, you know I am thinking, "What the fuck?"

"Don't worry, Mary, you are not entering a psychosis, or any of those other thoughts racing past right now."

"You sound like a doctor or something?"

"Well, I have seen a few ailments and cures go by."

"WHAT are you?"

"I am what you see. I am a tree."

"Great. I am talking to a fucking tree," I said with my mouth. I felt less crazy doing that even though it'd seem absolutely crazy to a sudden passerby, because I was talking to myself, which, by the way, can look crazy too. *I don't stand a chance. I feel crazy either way.*

"Yes, a tree is my form. You are a form. We are both alive. We are two life forms communicating with each other."

I couldn't believe some corner of me was finding this okay, even believable on some level.

"I know you are questioning your sanity, the believability of this. It is very, very real but not in the concrete way you are accustomed to. I know you know the human brain has a vast network of ability. So does every living thing."

We both sat silent for a time. Him in patience, me in swirling thoughts. I spoke next. "I am not sure how to know I am not just crazy. Maybe sleep medication or the history of other pills are poorly interacting or have pickled my brain. Delusions can seem like reality."

"I can tell you something you don't know about these woods. You could find out if it's true."

Cocking my head, I replied, "I suppose that'd be helpful. Can I ask you something I don't know?"

"You can ask."

"Do you know who built the lean-to and the tree stand farther into the woods?"

"I probably do but I don't think it's information for you right now."

"Well that's what I would *like* to know." I thought for a moment. "Can you tell me if I should feel fearful of that person?"

"No. You don't need to be fearful. Here's something you can check. These woods used to be a major thoroughfare for inhabitants moving between the South, getting to the North, and back in the 1860s. That is something you don't know about this place that you can check into. I understand this is much to take in, and you need time to check the information. I sincerely hope you do and that you return soon. I haven't had such hope in some time."

Was he talking about the Underground Railroad? A bit confused, I asked, "Hope in what?"

"For a human to serve as a conduit of information. There is so much to say, but let's take it one step at a time."

Standing up slowly since I'd sat with my legs folded for a long time, I looked at Cowboy and asked, "Do you have a name? Cowboy suddenly seems a bit insulting or demeaning."

"I wasn't insulted, it is the human representation I have chosen. I can explain more about that another time. My name is Populus Tremulous. I am pleased you asked."

"It may take some time for me to track down the information you gave, but I believe I will be back. One more thing: What about the others I see. They are real too?"

"Yes, very. Ask them. They will know it's okay now. They have other names but they actually like your take on them. You see them for who they are; so much better than most."

I smiled gently. I felt I'd been handed a gift. I felt eager to go. I thought I'd head to the lean-to after that, but I was eager to see if my delusion extended beyond Cowboy, or Warrior. After a short distance, I turned and said, "As each moment passes and I wrap my head around this, I very much hope I will be back too. See you, Popu ... whatever ... Cowboy."

"Bye, Mary. I am glad you are open and that I decided correctly."

With a final glance, I turned to look at Pop ... Tre ... Cowboy ... it was too many syllables. He was the same, no shifting of movement, but I felt a smile and heard a sigh of satisfaction. The fireflies were gone.

God, I thought I was preoccupied walking out after thinking I'd heard a person. That had nothing on this. I got to Warrior and stopped. I hadn't really noticed before that he was the remains of a pine tree.

I didn't "hear" any communication from him. Maybe he couldn't, being broken. Maybe it wasn't his job. Maybe he didn't want to speak yet.

As I gazed, I thought, "Thanks for your guidance," and then kept moving. My arm warmed as I moved away. I reached Tree Matt and found myself enjoying his lightness as I gazed at him.

Thanks for being my introduction. "I feel like I know you best," I directed my thought his way. No response, but I perceived a wink.

Maybe I was making this up. I definitely would be checking out the library. I thought that's where I could find the history of the woods. Proving to myself I was not wacky would be very comforting.

Chapter 16

I RAN INTO MATT'S FOSTER MOM AGAIN AS SHE was heading upstairs. She asked how things were in the woods. How she knew I'd been there, I wasn't sure. Maybe I smelled or something. I was quite sure that experience got some pheromones going. "Bella, right?" She nodded. "I am curious, do you have any idea how long the woods have been there? I am not even sure how long these apartments have been here."

"The apartments are from the seventies. It was more rural in general out here, I suppose. I have been back here five years and have seen much building go on."

She asked if I might want to come up for a cup of tea, or something a little stronger, a glass of wine, maybe. I surprised myself by saying yes.

"Number 208, right?" She nodded yes.

"Let me put away my pack and pee, then I will be up." I dropped it off, gave Tequila a brief stroking of her back, which caused her to hunch her rear. I told her, "I promise I'll be back soon." She protested with a strong meow and followed me to the door, so I reassured her of my quick return.

I went upstairs and knocked. Matt answered the door, clearly happy to see me, or maybe he was just happy to see any company. He invited me in. I was not sure I had ever seen as many plants as I could see at that moment. Healthy, thriving plants with deep vivid greens, yellows. Even a lemon tree. The apartment definitely got sun much of the day.

"Wow. A botanical garden in my complex, I had no idea."

"Yeah, some people have stray dogs or cats dropped off where they can't be rejected. I have plants. I do have a green thumb. We have a mutual admiration society going on."

"Between whom? You and Matt?"

"No, the plants and me. They get excited when they are carried in on their last stem or leaf."

"How do you know that?"

"I feel it. It's as if they survived long enough to reach the ER. I should start to re-home some of them, but they each bring joy. I am not sure who I could trust with them."

Matt chimed in, "I have learned so much about plants living here. I think my first job might be in a nursery or greenhouse."

"So, you like plants, Matt?"

"I didn't know I did. I confess, it seemed a bit bizarro when I first moved here. After a while, they do become comfortable to be with." As he was speaking, he was mindlessly but slowly stroking a smooth leaf of one of the few plants I can name, Bird's Nest plant.

Bella came over with a glass of wine, a healthy pour, at that.

"Hope you like red. It's all I keep around."

I smiled. "Perfect … I might have said that for a glass of white, but I wouldn't have meant it." Sipping wasn't my usual MO, but I gave the illusion that it was. We small-talked about my work and what Matt was studying in school. He said they had just finished up the conquistadors and were beginning the American colonies era. He felt more of a connection with that so far.

Speaking as if freshly read, Matt expanded, "The horribleness of conquering the natives of the Americas by conquistadors just isn't cool anymore." He was so very right. It's our history, but just because it happened doesn't mean it needs glorifying.

Bella asked about my background and what brought me to this

complex. I quickly explained the divorce, giving just the glossed-over version about poor communication, growing apart in interests. We needed to know each other much longer to go into the deeper version of infertility stress and beyond. I indicated affordability influenced the apartment choice, even though some were closer to work. Glancing out the window and pointing, I added, "The view of the woods sold me on it though. Seemed calming right away. I definitely needed that."

I asked Bella if she had been a foster mom for a long time. "Most of the five years I have been here. I confess, I needed some added income when I got here. Someone suggested it to me, thinking if I loved at-risk plants, maybe I'd be good with kids at risk. I discovered I was good at it, but even more that I loved it. In some ways, at-risk anything just needs nurturing, a willingness to listen, and not a hurried response." Shifting her gaze to Matt, she said, "Matt was easy though." Then she asked, "Do you mind if I tell her just the basics?"

"No, it's old news to me."

"Matt is easier because he knows his mom loves him and at some point, hopefully, can return. She has addiction issues, did some time, and is in rehab to be followed by halfway housing for transition. It was precarious for some time prior, it seems. She looked at him, "I do wish there were more kids around here for you to connect with, but you seem content." Ending with a bit of a questioning inflection.

"Woods, books, and video games. I am pretty lucky. I am so much happier than where I spent the first month with four other foster kids."

I finished my last sip without looking like I wanted to lick the glass. I thanked Bella and told Matt that hopefully we will solve the mystery of the cairns. Bella asked about the mystery, and when I finished telling her, she dismissed it and thanked me for joining her, adding, "I don't get out to socialize often."

Ahhhh, so nice, only had to walk down a flight of stairs to be home.

My mind returned to whether the woods being used for the Underground Railroad could be true. I got into my pajamas, grabbed a few nuts since I shouldn't take my medication on an empty stomach, and went to bed.

The next morning, I made it to work in record time. The day went smoothly, but I was very preoccupied with hitting the library after work to check out my level of sanity or insanity, whichever the case may be. I wasn't much into acting like I cared about every little thing at that point. *If the information checks out, how do I reconcile with the new truth. A tree frickin' talked to me.*

When I arrived at the library, there were only a few people inside. A couple school kids in the back were snuggling up, pretending to study. One person was online, while another perused a section of books. I asked the librarian if there were books or documents about the history of the region. She asked what time frame, what kind of history. After I clarified, she directed me to some old, archived newspapers but wasn't sure exactly where else I would find out about the Underground Railroad in our area. Even if it was accurate, it occurred to me that no local newspaper of the time was going to reveal the path of the URR. I decided I had to locate a black history expert who knew this area.

So, it is true. The Underground Railroad did travel through this part of the county. Shit, I know I didn't know that before right now. It's not like I could have projected that information from my brain. Now what do I do?

I got home and opened a beer. I needed to sit and sort this out in my head. *If a tree could talk, why would it WANT to talk to me?*

I fell asleep, but as usual, I woke up at three. Didn't need to get up until seven. *Of course, I wake up early when I could sleep a bit longer.* I decided to try journaling in hopes I could be back asleep by four. If I could persist through a few pages, I often uncovered the real issue.

Entry: I can't believe I think a tree talked to me. I walked in thinking the person would show up, reveal themselves. I surely didn't expect what I got instead. I thought I'd find out who made the lean-to, maybe a little piece of me thought I'd meet a current version hunk of a survivalist and we'd move to the woods. Some stupid story like that ... page 2, page 3 ... As a Speech Pathologist, I know human brains have such capacity for reasoning. I know trees are a living entity. I believe some people are psychic and can help sense what is deep inside of someone. I actually do believe that tree Populus Trem-something talked to me. But I am back to asking why it would talk to ME? More than anything, what is going to be asked of me? Why would it bother to seek me out? Why me? What does it ... he, the woods want? What might he ask me to do? Ahh, there we go, BINGO. It's not that I think I am crazy. It's not that it seems impossible to communicate with non-human sentient beings; it's about what responsibility is going to be put on me now? What was it he said, "I am glad I decided correctly." "Let's take this one step at a time." Those are the words that have me wondering. I am thinking "deciding correctly and one step at a time" means there's more. That's what they say at work when they pour new shit on you and try to prevent you from freaking out. "Let's take this one step at a time." Never seems to carry a great connotation for the person having to learn those steps. Now what do I do? What do I do next? 3:30 a.m. I will try to sleep. Get back in there depending on when I get out of work. If not, Saturday for sure.

Chapter 17

It was my third session with Hazel. She was showing signs of understanding more words, especially with substantial pause time for response and lots of visuals. *God, that is good to see. Not much is worse in my book than global aphasia. Somewhat like being able to move but being locked inside, plus locked out. Inside with your own ideas, outside from being able to interact with the world.*

"Can you show me ...?" I asked, as I mentioned an item in the room. She slow pointed to it. "Yes," I said with a smile. "And where is ...?" She sighed a relief when I said, "Right again!" and she beamed on three out of three! I couldn't wait to talk with her family. It was such a scary time for spouses and children. Their mind zooms right to the worst case and the fear of losing who they know. Slowing their thinking down, helping them see each day's achievement as a ray of hope, was crucial for everyone's frame of mind. Educating them that when substantial progress occurred within the first couple months, we could only project the outcome. Some patients flew by the expectation, while others stalled out faster than anyone wanted. That's when it got sad and the family mourned for the person as they knew them, and felt forced to start planning for "What now?" Sometimes I've had to remind even *myself* not to go there. It's been crucial to give hope and belief to the patient to spur their perseverance. They must believe it will get better so they bring their best to every single session.

I could see Hazel's processing stamina was waning. I'd hoped to go longer, but I could tell more words, more anything, would only start to swirl in her head like the leaves in a windstorm ... hard to grasp and to know what to latch on to. I knew I'd have to document why I was ending early, but I learned a long time ago that ending on the upswing would make her happy to see me tomorrow. Perhaps I needed to consider two short sessions a day versus one a day. I knew my supervisor would question why I didn't meet my "expected minutes." She had to ask because she would be asked by someone whose job it was to keep the numbers up and to comb for slacker patterns.

When I started in this setting, there was such a carefree attitude about our services. Camaraderie was amazing. We had such fun at work and with everyone. We could help CNAs; we could help nurses and actually talk with residents who weren't on our caseload. It was so much about relationships and quality time with patients. Then Medicare changes hit the fan and the shitstorm ensued. Productivity went from 50 or 60 percent to 90 or 95 percent. Sixty percent was somewhat low, but 75 to 80 percent would have been more manageable while still enjoying work. There were a slam of layoffs, with everyone wondering why one person was laid off while another stayed. Hours were cut, more group sessions were added, and we had to offer concurrent treatments. It normalized, but it never felt right. Maybe it was too lax before from a business standpoint, but soon it became a constant pressure with more focus on productivity and numbers, with lip service to the quality. I always knew when shit came from a couple levels up. It intensified on its way down. An undercurrent of panic would get communicated, and I'd walk away feeling like I must be doing something wrong if I couldn't manage the new intensity of the pace. I spent too much time blaming myself and minimizing my own organization, efficiency, and judgment.

Truth is, I was amazing. My patients made so much progress. I had a nurse at my last facility who sadly bid me goodbye with, "I have never seen so many patients get off tube feeding as you have accomplished." A high, high compliment from the director of nursing. Those were the days when outcomes rose way above numbers. Of course, we still had to show progress, but the nuances no longer mattered as they once had. Or should I say they mattered when they became an issue. When a family wasn't happy, then it mattered, and the Eye of Sauron's scrutiny turned to the clinician but not to the system that allowed so little time for family education and relationship building.

Burnout—that's what they called my affliction. I wasn't burned out with my field; I loved communication and Speech Pathology. I saw our oral communication and higher levels of thinking and reasoning as primary gifts that separate us from other sentient beings. *Other sentient beings. Communication. Reasoning. Is thinking this is a gift reserved for humans about to be turned upside down with recent events in the woods?* Burnout ... because I was too young to retire and had lots of years left but maybe had been working in the same area for too long. I'd seen procedures and policies introduced and then fade away just to resurface again in a pretty new package under the new management. The new management would be excited, but staff knew why it didn't work last time around. Still, I was expected to smile and jump in enthusiastically as the new grads were doing. I discovered it doesn't land well to point out it was tried ten years ago. Of course, it had a different name or different acronym. I wondered if there was a job where I could research old techniques and then think of new catchy acronyms for spinning the idea. It was one thing to change the documentation system as the privacy issues and technology expanded. It was another to change the work model as if it was better for patients, when clearly, it was the bottom line we were calculating it on.

I documented the minutes as they happened. How many articles had there been in the national association magazine over the years about the pressure to deliver and having to ignore the urge to pad minutes just to minimize the scrutiny? While that day's schedule with Hazel had been set, I scheduled two shorter sessions with her for the next day. It's what she needed, and it should also appease the gods watching vigil over my minutes.

Chapter 18

LETTING MY HEAD WANDER DOWN THAT RABBIT HOLE didn't make for a particularly great drive home. I was more surly than forgiving in traffic. I didn't have road rage in me, but I definitely had snarkiness in my straight-ahead stare, pretending I didn't see that turn signal. When I returned to my adult brain, I knew the strange sense of power I derived in those moments was pathetic. Dragged down by my own negativity, my body, likewise, dragged down the hall to my apartment. I could hear Tequila greeting me as I unlocked the door. She liked the treat she got for protecting the land. How she knew it was me and not another, I was not sure. *Would she expect the same treat from an intruder? Or might she leap on their head from the cabinet, claws extended?*

I sat on the patio, chewing on both a salad and the message of the woods. I decided to re-read my journal entry in the daylight and see if the troubled entry still made sense and resonated. My amethyst was sitting inside the door where I'd left it when I unpacked my pack before going to Bella's apartment. I rolled it around as I read the words. "What do they want? What will I be asked to do? and Why me?" Thinking back to that surprising pearl during the earlier in-my-head tirade, I wondered, *How do non-human sentient beings communicate, and can they reason? Maybe the human's definition of reasoning is wrong.*

I needed to move, to push the day's energy from my body. I knew tomorrow I would return to the woods, but at this time, I wanted to think nothing. I switched to my bike clothes. *Really need to get my bike off the trainer and outside. Maybe in a week or so. Weather could still turn shitty.* These days I was still enjoying rediscovering my iPod music. I hopped on and swung through the playlist. I heard Sara B, that's what I called her now, singing *Brave.*

I reconnected with my pride from that day with Barbara. My words had come out, I had a moment of what felt like bravery. It probably shouldn't be about Barbara or me. It should be about George, the patient, but that was the day the earth tilted on its axis toward me, versus away.

George was in the hospital with a substantial case of pneumonia. I definitely hoped he would recover but wondered if he'd make his way back to our facility or not. The debriefing analysis of that scenario had finally settled with the impact of patient compliance more than my or Barbara's response. Thank God it did result in improving how a patient's need for thickened liquids got communicated, so there were more checks in place.

I backed up to, *Believe It* by Cimorelli. These songs just kept giving. From believing in myself to stepping out of the shadows, believing I was capable of inspiring another. Not sure who all was traveling with me but I had met some intriguing people.

Brave was my song. Something was telling me *Believe It* was now also my song, or maybe after tomorrow it would be.

Chapter 19

I TRIED THE COLD WATER OPEN-MY-MIND SHOWER THING. I found myself letting the cold water hit my toes as I stood at the farthest reaches of
the shower. Time was interminable. I anxiously awaited the warm
water to work its way up the pipes. As I immersed myself in the
warmth that finally arrived, I was thinking about another dabbler
topic that was trendy a few years back. The messages in water. A
mentor had talked about visions when standing in water; another
talked about drinking a glass of water before bed while considering
an issue to stimulate a dream. For me, it'd only stimulate getting
out of bed in the middle of the night to pee.

I put a full lunch in my pack, thinking I might spend longer in the
woods today. Filled a Nalgene bottle with water and grabbed the book
Ishmael too. Maybe reminding myself about a wise gorilla that speaks
would make me feel less apprehensive. Even though I told myself I
wasn't scared about what I was stepping into, the old "Boy Scout"
mindset told me to toss in my Swiss Army knife and whistle. "Plan for
the worst, hope for the best"—I thought those were Dale Carnegie's
words. I placed my amethyst in the possibility pouch and grabbed my
sitting pad.

I left the apartment, and soon the sounds of cars gave way to a large gathering of birds in the trees as I entered the woods. *Is it mating season, or merely a lively discussion about the best way to build birds' nests? Why don't more people walk here? I am glad I can feel these woods belong to me, but it's hard for me to fathom why people stay in the noise so much.*

My meditating was lasting longer but wasn't yet a pleasure. I sat for a while looking at Cowboy. Nothing was happening. I checked my watch; ten minutes had passed. Then twenty minutes. That was reaching my capacity.

"I said I'd be back. Here I am." Nothing happened. *Oh lovely, I was imagining it, I am crazy.* As I was thinking that the leaves emerging on the surrounding trees swayed, I heard a gentle, low-pitched humming sound. The fireflies floated past my hair. I knew I shouldn't be able to see their illumination in the daytime, but here it was. Almost like dew drops on leaves as the sun spanned the trees.

With a little irritation, I said, "Does this mean you are finally going to talk to me?" Guess I'd slid right from disbelief to expectation on the tree-talking meter.

Sounding much wiser and more patient, Cowboy said, "I am glad to see you return."

"Was it a test to see how long I would sit here?"

"No, no test. We are working around the world. I was in what you may call a meeting."

"There's others like you?" I wondered.

"As well as others like you."

My feeling of superiority took a step back. "Others like me. Others you talk to, or that talk to trees?"

"Both, I have attempted before. There are others like you around the world who are waking to their possibility."

"What have you attempted? To talk ... to communicate with a human?"

"Yes."

"What happened to the others?"

"The first was long ago when we knew earth's composition was being disrupted, but humans weren't aware. The second was not so long ago, but the person stopped coming. I can only predict why. She never said specifically."

It was a woman then. "What do you predict?"

"Fear. Doesn't that stop so many things? Fear within or without."

A scene from *Mission: Impossible* popped into my head: *"Your mission, if you should decide to accept it ..."*

"Do you ever see her?" I asked.

"Rarely comes this way."

"But she visits the woods?"

"So, I hear from others."

Smirking, I replied, "You are not a tree of many words."

"It takes some energy, as you can imagine, to do this. Conserving is a good thing."

My smirk changed to appreciation. "Why you? Why are you the communicator when you are not the only face I see?"

"I am the elder. The energy or power takes time to build, to develop."

"How old are you?"

"155."

"I noticed the engraving of 1938 on your trunk. I didn't know any trees but sequoias and ponderosas lived so long."

"I am nearing the end of my thriving years. The system will continue. It is strong for now."

"Why do you say for now?" I asked.

"The world is changing. There are many precarious junctures reaching critical points."

"What do you want from me?"

"That is for you to determine."

I scoffed an overly incredulous, "What!?"

"It's not for me to tell you what you need to do, for I do not know."

Sensing panic but not sure of its source, I began, "First I was worried I was crazy, but then I realized I was worried about what would be asked of me. You are saying I don't have an 'assignment,' a task?"

"You may have a task. I hope you have a task, but I cannot assign it; it is for you to discover."

A sense of pressure was swarming me. I could hear the cadence of my voice escalating. "So, you hope I will do something, but you don't know what it is, or you can't tell me what it is?"

With a cadence opposite of mine, he calmly reminded me, "I am sure you have experienced knowing you needed help without being able to define what form of help you need. This forest's essence senses that need for help and we reached out so another may discover the path."

Standing and putting my arms through the loops of my pack, I nodded and said, "I do understand that statement. People outside myself saw my ache after my divorce and offered to help in ways I didn't know to ask for. I continue to be doubtful I have the answers." Inhaling deeply, I said, "No offense, but I need to walk." Flicking a hand in a helpless goodbye, I started back down the path.

I saw Warrior Man staring at me as I cut off from the path. Did he look sad or was he reflecting my feelings? Just sensed a shift in his one eye.

I got back to the lean-to. No one was there. I figured Matt had to be in school. I stared up at the tree stand. I found the ankle hook in two sways. Each handhold on the ladder later became a foothold; only the first move required a near-dynamic thrust. The pack added a few off-kilter pounds, but soon I was on the platform. I knew it was only twenty feet up, but the perspective was a welcomed change. It was embedded in the branches just enough so you wouldn't see it unless you gazed up. A glance would cause it to go unnoticed. Interestingly, there was a clear line to the lean-to.

Opening my pack, I snacked on some gorp. I guess the scent was floating through the branches, because I saw a squirrel drop from a higher branch and scamper along a branch toward me with its cackling plea for sharing. I momentarily envisioned this rabid squirrel leaping at me, but I squelched my paranoia. I pulled out *Ishmael*. I fanned the pages, seeing the dozens of dog-eared pages. It was how I read. Something triggered an "aha" or showed me something I'd never imagined, and it got dog-eared. There was so much of that in this book. I read a passage.

I woke up abruptly, thrusting my back against the tree and reflexively shooting forward. I noticed the sun beaming on my feet. Then another pebble hit the platform. I couldn't track its origin. Can't be from above, so I looked down and saw Bella below.

Glad to see her, I joked, "Hey, you could hurt someone."

"I doubt the pebble is going to do harm, but you are in my loft."

"Your loft! You built this?"

"Yes, and the lean-to." She scurried up the ladder, obviously having been up many times. There was barely room for us both, but we sat silently beside each other, looking across into the branches.

Finally, I said, "I guess my first question is, how did you learn to build forts?"

"My ex was a skilled craftsman. If I wanted to spend time with him, then I watched and learned how to create from wood."

"But why the survival fort?"

"Ultimately, this place was literally for my survival, mental more than physical. After the divorce, the reality of regret and loneliness was consuming, and I needed a place for solitude that didn't include four walls, each written with a reminder of what went wrong."

"Ugh. Well put. I can understand some of your angst and agree the forest's energy is a savior. How long ago was that?"

"Five years."

"I guess your squatter's rights do supersede my own."

"I have barely been here for the past two years until I felt beckoned back the last several months."

Making the connection, I asked, "So Matt doesn't even know you come back here?"

"No, I have stayed quiet. I wanted him to find the solace of the place, feel something was his. I also felt a need to make sure it was safe. When I started returning, I noticed an added stone to the cairn. I knew someone else was coming. I was surmising it was you but wanted to be sure."

"I was envisioning something much more romantic coming from the cairn than my neighbor, but the mystery is solved."

School was going to let out soon, and Bella liked to be there to greet

Matt. Something he didn't have in his home life. We climbed down, which was still scarier than it sounded, given the swaying rope ladder. No issue for Bella.

We parted ways at the Warrior. She didn't say anything or seem to notice. She didn't ask where I was going, or why. *Guess she's not one who is awakened to them.* I got back to Cowboy, pulled out my mat once again, and sat there looking at him with an intention.

"If you can't tell me what I need to do, can you tell me more about what you need? Can you tell me why you 'approached' me?" I felt the slight breeze and knew the fireflies would be on them. They encircled Cowboy.

"It's not me, it's we. The collective of the earth, the collective of growing sentient beings that are fewer than at my seedling time. The soil we thrive in, the soil we need, is waning in its life force. We are in danger. If we are in danger, humans are not far behind."

"I know about climate change, but in danger how?"

"The soil nutrients have diminished so we have less to go around. Soon we all will be undernourished. Our energy is fading."

"Are you dying?"

"I am old. I have lived past what most do. I need to give back to the soil, so others flourish. I am not referring to me as one. Do you know about an aspen's life span?"

"Not really. Y'all seem to be here, and every now and then, one seems to blow over or leaves stop returning."

"I am at the long end of my cycle. I was a seedling in 1865. Did you check on my information?"

With an excited gasp, I replied, "Yes! Can't believe I didn't start with that! The Underground Railroad did run through here. So, you knew that because you were growing that far back! Does that have something to do with why I see you as Cowboy?"

"Yes, we all take on the persona of the era of our seedling."

"Warrior Man? Certainly, he was a seedling during a major war. Matt, based on that, must be the 1950s or '60s maybe?"

"Yes, I needed you to believe in my existence, but I also need you to believe in you."

I queried, "Why did you approach me and 'wake up' to me?"

"You are a communicator. You think it's only your job, but you know it courses through your veins." I just sat quietly as he paused. My mind was drifting back to *What's he going to ask me to do? What responsibility am I taking on?*

He continued, "Aspens grow in clones. We share a root structure and have identical characteristics."

Still, I questioned my ability. "I am not sure how I can help. I know nothing about botany. I operate best one-to-one, and even then, persuasion has never been my gift. Others with idiotic ideas get followed because they can say something better, even if their message is wrong. Not sure how I can gather others to help you."

"These woods have talked about you for a while. You are more than you know."

With yet further resistance, I said, "You want me to help you, but you can't tell me how, but whatever it is, it's going to help the world."

"You put the 'world' spin on it, not me."

Acknowledging but changing the direction of this, I said, "I met the person who built the lean-to. Turns out I knew her already! Certainly not someone to fear."

"Did she speak of her woods experience?"

"No, why?"

He was silent. After a bit, he broke the silence with, "You have much to consider."

Still not seeing my path forward, I pushed further by asking, "What do I tell people, 'This tree told me other trees need help'?"

Ignoring my resistance, Cowboy clarified, "Well more specifically, our soil … You help many that others would give up on. As I said, you are more than you know. The responsibility you fear doesn't feel so heavy when it's the right time for others to join. There is a collective thought in the works."

Blowing out a sigh, I replied, "It's surely been a day. I guess I will head out. I should have brought a beer with me instead of just water."

"Beer is even good for the soil," he said. I felt a smile and a wink.

Chapter 20

I HADN'T REALIZED HOW MUCH TIME HAD PASSED, BUT it explained why I was hungry. I hadn't eaten my sandwich, so I sat on the patio with Tequila, who was hoping for a morsel of something she wasn't supposed to have. I Googled beer's benefits for soil. *Damn, that tree knows what he's talking about.*

Stale beer has yeast, proteins, sugars, and other beneficial nutrients like potassium, calcium, magnesium, phosphorus, and more. Beer also has carbs, which feed the microbes in the soil, which in turn feed the plants. After sitting out overnight, the alcohol evaporates.

Tequila began rubbing her head across my arm with the mole. With all the weird shit going on, I felt a need to find out what was happening with the moles on my body. *Why am I so unconcerned? Should I be concerned and just stop procrastinating? Monday, I will call on Monday.*

I knocked on Bella's door. Matt opened it, as expected.

"Hey, Matt. Happy sunny Sunday. How are you?"

"Trying to do some math homework. I hate fractions. I liked the geometry unit so much better. I can 'see' it."

"Wish I could be of help. Is Bella here?"

"BELLA MOMMMMM. It's Mary!"

"Uhm, Matt, the apartment's pretty small, not sure shouting is necessary," I said with a curled silly lip. She came out, drying her hands from doing dishes, I guessed.

"Sorry to bother you on a Sunday, Bella. I just wondered if I could run something by you."

"No worries, I enjoy company. Too early for wine, want some iced tea?"

"Please." It was mint, refreshing for a Sunday morning. It occurred to me that I should have come bearing muffins or something. I scanned the kitchen, seeing a plant on nearly every surface. All healthy, deep colors.

"What's on your mind?" she asked.

"Not sure where to start. I have been going to the woods frequently these days. I know you used to. Did you ever sense anything there? Sense any communication?" There was a pause with her mouth starting to form a word, then stopping twice, followed by a deep breath and a sip of tea. "I am sorry," I said. "I am clearly making you uncomfortable."

Nervously, she asked, "What kind of communication are you suggesting?"

"Well," then blurting, "a tree."

She gave a slight exhale of relief. "Guess he didn't want to give up."

"Who's he, and give up what?" I asked.

"An old aspen, right?"

"Yeahhhh. Did it look like a cowboy or have wood eaten so the black spots look like a cowboy wearing a big hat?"

"No, it looked like a tree." Then she asked, "What does he want?"

"I am not completely sure," I said. "Help of some kind. The trees are at risk of dying. The soil is weak. He held back from specifics of what he hoped I'd do. I am still wrapping my head around it. So, what did he want from you?"

"We didn't get very far. Help of some kind, I suppose. I pretty much freaked out at the mere thought of a tree communicating with me. I was in a place that I was questioning most levels of my sanity, and I felt incapable of helping anyone else, let alone a tree, which was beyond my comprehension. He said I was not tuned into my 'gifts.' I never took the path that direction again."

"He told me a similar thing … 'You are more than you know.' He said they have been watching me for a while."

"They?"

My hands gestured wide open. "Yeah, there are sentry trees that have watched my movement, I guess, sizing up my … something. They send messages to the tree I call Cowboy, the old tree. I am just *so* relieved to hear you heard something too. I thought of you, one, because you are the only other person I know who uses the woods, except for Matt, of course. And two, because I figured your connection to plants is a similar thing. Now we know neither of us were crazy, at least not completely. Ha!"

Showing a reflective gaze, she said, "Interestingly, once I experienced and rejected that tree, now known as Cowboy, the next thing I knew, all these plants started entering my life. And he's right. The soil is their currency."

Chapter 21

MONDAY CAME TOO QUICKLY. I HADN'T SEEN LENA in forever. I hated it when I had that special patient who got discharged, but I knew I would keep in touch and check in on them forever, and the next thing I knew, weeks had gone by. Other cases took their place. But I WOULD see Lena on that day. I couldn't wait to tell her about the developments. I didn't even think she would view me as crazy.

I did check on Mr. Talbot, who was doing swimmingly with his regular diet. He needed to watch for fatigue and take smaller bites, but he would be ready for anything his wife put in front of him when he got home.

It was noon and I still hadn't called the doctor. *Just do it, now, you don't even need to call. Make an appointment online.* I switched from the documentation screen to the patient portal website. It was hard to get in with my primary, so I figured the nurse practitioner was a good place to start. I made an appointment for the next week, Thursday. *Perfect, more time to procrastinate or cancel.*

I popped into Lena's room. She was exuberant at my voice. She said, "I have heard it in the hall a few times, you're no quiet talker, but it fades away like the sound of a passing train."

"Oh, I know, I am so horrible. I can't stay now either, but I wanted to make sure I could share something with you later, maybe over dinner? I could request your tray be sent here instead of the dining room. I will see what they have, maybe I will get something too. How does that sound?"

"I can't wait! Been a long time since I had a dinner date! Will there be candlelight?"

"I think candles are against code, uhm, would you see it anyway?"

"No, but ambiance is something one can sense. Now get back to work," she said jokingly.

It helped that I had to interact with the kitchen staff so frequently. They didn't mind having me pick up Lena's meal and let me order dinner for myself. SLPs who work in schools are always told to make friends with the maintenance staff, and here, it's them and the kitchen staff. I told the CNA on second shift I'd be eating with Lena and would set the tray up as she asked.

"Dinner is served, madam," I said as I entered the room. "Lasagna!" she exclaimed as she was getting into her chair. I chimed in, "I know, I think it's one of their best dinners here." Lena was now able to get in and out of bed on her own, which opened up the world in a long-term care wing. Waiting for the loving but overworked CNAs to answer a call light sometimes led to poor patient choices. I set the tray up and oriented her to what and where it was.

"So, what was it you wanted to share? I have been curious all afternoon."

I began, "I have been practicing with the third eye concept. I have also read info. Not sure I am 'feeling' anything consistently, but I had a most unusual, definitely unexpected thing happen while in the woods." She nodded at me to go on. "I told you how I see the faces, much like you do. This is going to sound pretty unbelievable, but one of the trees talked to me." Her eyebrows raised, but her hand motioned me to keep going. "Well, that is the news. Doesn't it sound bizarre?"

"First, no not bizarre. Second, you must be very special to have been picked. Third, what did it say?"

"Why special?"

"I have only known one other who really heard the trees. It was an extremely special person. He's since passed. You are so much more than you know. So what did the tree say?"

I wish she could have seen the look on my face. "That's what the tree said! That I am more than I know!"

"Great minds think alike. So, what did it say besides that?"

I shared what the tree said about being old, dying, and the soil worn down. She sat with that for a moment.

"This has been brewing for decades. So much going wrong with the earth. You have a task ahead of you. You are going to take up the task, aren't you? You can't say no to such a plea."

"I don't know," I responded. "I have no idea about any of this. I read enough that I know the earth is in trouble. I have never wanted or expected to be an activist. I wouldn't even know where to begin." After a pause, I continued, "Not sure my frame of mind even wants an added responsibility. It's exciting on one hand, but I feel worn down from work most days. How would I save trees? Not sure I want to take on anything new. Sure, I feel bad about the world, the earth, but people smarter than me have not been able to slow it. I go into the woods for peace and solace, not to be put to work."

Adding wisdom and perspective, she advised, "You are thinking you have to dive in and fix things in a month. Maybe the tree just needs someone to listen, pay attention, believe, start a dialogue. You said it's not telling you what to do. It's not putting pressure on you; you are projecting that on yourself."

As she was speaking, she rubbed her hand over the mole on my arm, and added, "I am not concerned with it anymore; it feels like part of you."

"Maybe," I said, but I have an appointment soon to have it looked at. For some reason, I am not concerned either. Just don't want to be stupid. I have seen a couple people who ignored symptoms and changes, and ended up very sorry." I was picturing the woman I saw as I passed her room, who had a cavity where her nose had been. A sad memory imprinted forever.

"I need to be heading out. Thanks for listening and sharing dinner,

Lena. It may be wrong to think this, but I am secretly glad you weren't able to leave here."

"It's wonderful getting to know you too. Although familiar and filled with life memories, it was pretty lonely at home anyway. Maybe just keep talking to the tree. Things may become clearer over time. I doubt you have to save the world by next week."

That statement did release a bit of steam off the pot. I squeezed her hand and said it wouldn't be so long before my next visit. I hoped it would be true.

I'm not sure why I didn't go back to Cowboy, but I didn't. Not right away. What Lena said about spending more time in the woods made sense. I had uploaded a song on my phone, and once I got deeper in, I pulled out my earbuds and started playing *I Talk to the Trees* by Clint Eastwood. My mom loved the old movie *Paint Your Wagon*. She would sometimes sing the song around the house and definitely when we walked. It became an annoying joke that was sure to make us laugh.

I got to Tree Matt. On a whim, I went up and hugged him. I glanced around. I rarely saw people, but I figured with my luck, this would be the moment someone would happen by. It wasn't a quick hug; it lasted and lasted. I ran my hand along the roughness of his bark. Aspens look so smooth from a distance. Leaning back from him, but my hands still touching, I scanned the face I'd see from the path. I could see sharp ridges of bark made up his black hair and the gouges made up the center of his round eyes. I gave him one last wraparound hug and looked into the woods. I felt light, and I ran to another tree and hugged that one. Then another. I startled a squirrel who scurried higher up the tree but then just stood upside down staring at me, not knowing if I was friend or foe.

I restarted the song and started humming, then quietly sang the words. I was imitating Clint Eastwood's wandering gait stepping over branches, swinging up, and walking along downed logs. His voice coming right into my ears emboldened me. Suddenly believing I could carry a tune, I got louder, and my voice was bellowing through the woods. I was smiling, singing, and high-fiving every tree I came near. Just like how one song links your brain to another, I thought of

Julie Andrews singing *The Hills Are Alive.* I felt a lightness of spirit I couldn't recall having, maybe ever. The kind of lightness a child must have when they're in the yard pretending to be a superhero or doing cheers for an imaginary crowd.

The song was on loop, but eventually, I drew in a deep, reflexive breath and let out a massive releasing sigh. I stopped the song and looked around. I noticed the leaves having different variations among the same trees. I saw plants growing on the forest floor, with smaller companion plants beside the larger ones. I saw a bird bobbing in a small puddle that remained from some recent rain. I headed back toward the path. I needed to see Warrior Man. I slapped Matt on the back in an old Captain Kirk fashion, and said, "Thanks for opening your part of the woods to me." I hurried down the path.

I plopped, sitting on my downed warrior. I scanned his patched eye and wondered what caused that. His lined and weathered face was both frightening and protective. He must be seen differently by all who actually notice him. Or does he decide the intended face that others see?

I need some of your strength. Something is happening I don't understand, but I believe I will need an infusion of warrior spirit. You look as if you have witnessed war and weathered storms.

I sat a few more minutes, listening to my breath move in and out. Feeling it on the back of my throat, a calmness washed over me. *I guess I am ready.* I looked around the woods once more and stood, heading on to Cowboy. I walked very methodically, consciously either in avoidance or a walking meditation mode. It didn't matter which. I was walking.

I didn't have my pad with me. I had left the apartment without an intention of the day, so I hadn't prepared and only brought a little water. It didn't matter. The sun was out and had warmed my usual spot. When I sat, I slipped off my shoes and rubbed my bare feet slowly across the dirt. I had always wished I enjoyed walking barefoot. I was amazed when I saw the dirty soles of a person's feet that told me they spend much of their day shoeless. At that moment, I may have experienced some of their delight. The small pebbles massaged the bottom of my feet. I burrowed like I was on the sandy beach, enjoying the work my toes and heels were doing.

I heard the low pitch of the breeze coming closer through the branches. Soon the fireflies were floating past my head and gathering in such an honoring way on Cowboy's ten-gallon hat. I knew what was next.

As if stretching, he started slowly, "You seem both serene and nervous, Mary. Should I feel worried I have caused you such discomfort? You were the hum of the woods this morning, bringing delight, and I am pleased to say, you are back sooner than I expected."

"I have a wise friend who advised I should just spend time out here. Talk more with you but not to feel I have to take up some quest today."

"That is a wise friend. I don't intend to pressure, or direct. I'm just hopeful you will be the one who wakes other people, causing a tide to begin."

Moving my mouth sideways, I stated, "Not sure that alleviates my pressure, but I am here. What is happening to your ... our soil? Why is it a problem?"

"Settled agriculture has been occurring for ten thousand years. Tools to plant and harvest were initially seen about 5000 BC. Plowing with oxen was relatively benign. Over the years, the expanses of land became disturbed by heavy machines that compact the soil with their weight and routinely plow, turning over six or seven inches of soil. Nothing in nature's routine turns over that volume of soil. Standard farming clears the land of healthy but human-scorned debris. Exposed to the air, previously stored CO_2 is released to the atmosphere."

"But farming is needed to feed the world."

"True, but the diminished soil quality, along with the release of carbon, and very few restorative practices, are leaving soil with fewer nutrients for the food that's grown. Then enter the manufacturers of products that further degrade the soil. It's reaching a critical mass."

Chapter 22

WHEN THURSDAY ARRIVED, I LEFT WORK EARLY TO go to the doctor. I thought about canceling but decided I could quell the health care provider in me by going. It was a warm day, so I was wearing a short-sleeved shirt. I sat in the exam room waiting for the nurse practitioner, my hand gliding over the mole. It felt satiny, not rough. It resembled something but I couldn't think what.

"Hi Ms. Keeley. I am Melinda. What can I do for you today?" *I hate when they ask that. Is it a test to see if I am going to say the same thing I claimed when I made the appointment?*

She washed her hands while I explained, "I have had this mole, and another on my leg appeared a couple months ago. They haven't really grown. My sense is they are nothing but thought I should check them out."

She pulled out her dermo scope and started inspecting the one on my arm. She probed it with a blunt pencil-looking object. She pinched it with her fingers. Pulling up, she slightly shrugged and said, "It doesn't have any markers of a cancer. I'd like to look at the other mole before deciding, but we have some options. We could scrape it for a biopsy, or I could send you to a dermatologist and let a specialist look at it."

She gave me privacy to change out of my pants. I hadn't noticed the other mole as much since it was usually covered. It had the same overall appearance of satiny. That one was round but had lines running through it. She returned to the room and lifted the sheet from the side to view my mole. She went through the same close exam and probing. She leaned back again and said, "I think it's unusual to get two new moles of this size as quickly as you did. However, neither look alarming nor even concerning to me. I would feel more comfortable if we scraped them, or you go to a dermatologist and have them checked."

I did not feel like bothering with the scraping process, so I said, "I will make an appointment with a dermatologist." I didn't really feel a sense of relief since I wasn't particularly worried anyway. Instead, it felt like something I was able to check off my to-do list.

The dermatologist basically said the same thing when I saw her a couple weeks later. I figured I'd had enough medical response to assuage future comments from concerned friends and colleagues. I still wasn't clear why Tequila was so darn interested in them, but maybe the raised area was like any convex surface, simply pleasant to rub.

I got home and found a small plant in a pretty little planter sitting by my door. There was no doubt where it had come from, but I chuckled at the sad life this little guy was entering. I envisioned it sobbing and flailing its little leaves as it was stripped from the comfort of its luscious community.

Hey there. I see someone thinks I need a project. I picked it up gently, holding it at eye level as I unlocked the door with my other hand. *I am quite sure you sense my novice level, but I will do my best. At least your family is close by.*

I texted Bella and thanked her but was sure to include a couple question marks and a "thinking" emoji. She texted back, telling me it was Matt's idea. "He said if you were good at helping out one foster child, you should have one of your own. Be glad he only considered a plant, and there wasn't a brooding teen at your door." She added a smiley face. *You get a glimpse of the power of addiction when it can cause someone to have such a sweetheart of a kid and still act in a way that puts them in jeopardy and fucks so extensively with their life.*

I set my new plant on the table and scanned the room. I knew Tequila's favorite spots. She might not appreciate my taking one of her warming platforms. I wanted to put it somewhere I frequently plant my own body, so it had to be by the patio door. I shifted a little table over and sat the plant down. The table had a large enough surface that the plant and Tequila could be together. *Instead of a companion plant, you have a companion cat.* I stood back and looked. *For rarely ever giving plants more than a passing thought, they sure are being thrust front and center right now.*

Chapter 23

I GOT A WHIM AND WENT TO THE NEARBY nursery to look for a water mister and maybe some plant fertilizer. I remember my mom telling me misting plants was a big thing in the seventies.

I found myself wandering around inside the warm greenhouse, even though I knew the misters and fertilizer were probably near the counter, not out here. The moist and warm humidity hugged my skin, sliding over it like lotion.

"Can I help you find something?" Her voice startled me as I was languishing in the warmth. I saw a woman with long blond hair. The kind that is straight after washing. Not the kind requiring the work that my wavy hair required to either get a decent curl or the shiny, straight look.

"No, I really came in for a small amount of fertilizer and for a plant mister. But I'm loving the warmth and the colors in here."

"Linger as long as you like. The plants probably enjoy it. I need to do some tending anyway and keep my eye on the register too."

Jokingly, I said, "You should have chairs out here for a place your customers can pause or escape into some peacefulness."

With an index finger to her chin, the woman smirked, "I hadn't really considered that before, but it definitely has appeal. However,

I also enjoy the solitude of my work. Don't often want people over-staying."

Hearing the bells to the main door jingle, she left. When she returned, she was carrying a folding chair. She opened it in front of the annuals and motioned for me to sit. "You look like there are things on your mind. Sit a bit and see what the plants have to offer about peace of mind."

I sat. I watched the petunias and another flower I loved but didn't know the name of it. When I looked at the stick, it said, Cosmos. It had delicate, almost crepe-paper-like petals in gorgeous pastels. I sat down again, listening to my breath as I studied the flowers. *They are not fighting, resisting, or judging. Just growing and adding beauty to the world. They live here happily only to withstand the elements and eventually die back. They leave without clinging to anything.* Not sure what that thought was about, but I thought I was relating to myself.

The woman worked her way back around to where I was sitting. "Ah, that looks better. Feel better?"

Shifting in the chair, I said, "I do, surprisingly, but I guess I should actually get the two things I walked in to buy." I stood up, preparing to fold the chair as she reached for it. Her arm brushed mine.

She glanced at my arm. "That's intriguing."

"What?" I followed her gaze. "My mole?"

Cocking her head, she said, "Is that what it is? It looks remarkably like a seed pod of a buckeye tree." I just stared at her. *Great, either I am going to end up with one of those novelty things like a birthmark resembling the face of Jesus, or even more wonderful, I am turning into a tree. I have seen one too many sci-fi movies. The Fly, District 9.* With a final thought, she added, "I imagine you have had it looked at?"

"Yes, nothing that has to be removed. I have a second mole that also showed up out of nowhere. I'd be curious what you think of that one. Maybe I will take a picture of it and come back sometime." I went inside where she helped me find a general fertilizer since I had no idea what my plant was. "I noticed your expression when I said the mole looked like a seed pod. I hope I didn't alarm you. Seems a mole resembling something in nature is better than what it could have been."

"Yeah, there has just been a series of peculiar events lately, and this is right in line with it. That was the reason your remark surprised me." Shrugging her shoulders, she said, "Maybe see it as an honor to have a connection to the earth in such a way. Or it's a metaphor for what you are giving life to."

"Both better thoughts than skin cancer. I do think I will come back with a picture. I am curious now. By the way, I am Mary. What's your name?"

"Portia. When you do return, feel free to build in some flower-gazing time too. They do like the admiration."

Naturally, as soon as I got home, I Googled the buckeye tree seed pod. Sure enough, my mole looked very similar. I Googled tree seed pods in general. Didn't see anything specific that resembled the one on my leg. Maybe it was just a coincidence. I won't be growing roots anytime soon. I grabbed my phone and took a photo of the mole anyway. *I am sure I will get back there soon.*

It took a couple weeks, but I got back to the nursery. I was hopeful Portia was working when I got there. Seeing her, I approached. "Hi, hope you remember me."

"Sure I do. I pondered the message of your mole for much of that day. How are you, Mary?"

"I am good. I have the picture on my phone." As I looked around admiring the warmth of the place, I asked, "Do you own this place?"

"Yeah, I bought it a couple years ago after I decided I wasn't doing anything productive with my botany degree."

"Oh, so that's why my mole triggered an immediate thought," I said. I pulled out my phone and swiped through my photos until I found it and enlarged it.

Her eyebrows quickly and slightly rose when I showed it to her. "What do you think?"

"This mole is very different from the other."

"Yes." It was a bit rougher with almost imperceptible lines criss-crossing through it.

"It doesn't look like a seed pod. Just as interesting, it looks like a knot in a tree."

Chapter 24

I WENT AND SAT AT THE TREE. I WAITED patiently, feeling confident Cowboy would start soon. It'd been awhile. I was about ready to give up when I felt the breeze. Gentle, as if someone was slowly blowing on my cheek.

Gazing at Cowboy, I said, "I came back just to get more details about what you see as the concern for the soil."

"I can really only re-emphasize the same. The soil in so many places isn't healthy anymore. There was a time when there was a symbiotic relationship between air and earth. Earth stored carbon and trees gave people oxygen. Ancient cultures had farming practices that better served the earth than those being used now."

"What is different?"

"The soil is overused. It's left bare to erode. Fertilizer is killing microbes that help store carbon. Current large-scale farming practices are impacting the storage of carbon. It's lost or released half of its carbon over the centuries since agriculture began. Of course, all living creatures have to eat, including animals and plants. We can't change how many people are on this earth. Since humans insist on needing to consume animals, we can manage them differently. Methods of farming can be changed. It's not too late."

Beginning to recognize that I was always questioning, I asked, "How can farming be changed? There are billions to feed?"

"One simple, uncomplicated method is cover crops."

Dipping my head and looking sideways, I said, "Those are …?"

"They are crops sown by farmers between market crops to protect bare soil from wind and rain erosion. Agronomics. My friends tell me it's a practice as old as the Roman Empire. The practice of monocultures is reducing the biodiversity of the land. All of this destroys the soil integrity. Large amounts of carbon get released into the air."

"So, I am extrapolating, it ends up contributing to global warming?"

"Yes. It all disrupts the soil's communities of microorganisms that store the carbon. They have been begging me to find someone who can tell the humans."

"Not doubting you so much, but exactly how do microorganisms beg?"

"Death is very persuasive. There are many avenues underground."

I found myself remembering Ishmael's statement about being able to speak in a manner the human understood. I was even tiring of this question myself, but still I asked, "At the risk of being repetitive, you think I am the answer?"

"Hopefully, part of the answer," Cowboy said.

"Bella, the person you said you'd sought out before, actually lives where I do."

"I certainly find people of similar thought often end up neighboring."

"She said she wasn't ready and maybe you freaked her out."

I perceived a chuckle before Cowboy said, "Communicating trees can have that effect, I suppose."

Chapter 25

I GOT HOME AND THE MAGAZINE FROM NATURAL GROCERS was in the mail. The main article was, "Can Regenerative Agriculture Help Save the Planet." *Does the universe change my mail based on my ongoing thinking? It's like a newspaper arriving by owl to Harry Potter, or the pictures from* Back to the Future *changing based on actions.*

It described something called regenerative agriculture, which supports the use of cover crops. I read that healthy soil makes crops more resilient to extreme weather like droughts and helps farmland recover more quickly from extreme weather events. Then healthy soil can act as a carbon sink with the ability to sequester large amounts of CO_2 from the atmosphere. *Sequester, I like that term. Only heard it as a negative before, such as with a jury.* The article continued referring to the importance of livestock in the soil quality equation, "When animals are grazed in a way that mimics a natural ecosystem of grazing and regular movement they are able to restore degraded grasslands to the full capacity to sequester CO_2."

I started Googling. Agriculture production is currently the planet's largest use of land, occupying about 40 percent of the earth's land surface and responsible for 25 percent of the global greenhouse gas emissions, according to a 2019 report from the UN Environment Program

(UNEP). *That's a wake-up number for sure! Agriculture takes up 40 percent of the land on earth! Good news, I guess it's only responsible for one-quarter of greenhouse emissions.* I liked this statement by Project Drawdown, a global research organization: "The world cannot be fed unless the soil is fed."

On my next visit to the woods, I wanted to find out more about Cowboy. "Why do the fireflies come every time before you talk to me?"

"As I have said, I am old. I am dying. They help provide some strength."

"How do you call them?"

"I don't, you do." My mouth was poised to interject, but he kept talking. "Before you say you don't call them, let me explain. They feel your energy in the forest. They know I have reached out to you. They know I need assistance to communicate, and they are happy to lend some strength."

"All the times I saw fireflies on summer nights growing up, did they have this power?"

Cowboy said, "Some are just beings. No particular gift. Some have added skill to lend, others just live."

"Sounds like the world. I looked up some information about the earth, the soil. Soil depletion is on many people's radar, apparently, and now it's on mine. Not sure why you grabbed me with all the knowledgeable people out there. Wrong person in the right place, or wrong person in the wrong place?"

"Remember, I said you are a communicator. Not everyone is. You haven't tapped into much of what you can do. That I sense. People you are referring to are scientists, but more people are entering awareness. I hope you will gather some of those people."

"I am loving your belief in me, but what you see in me is not the same as my being able to impact any solution."

"As long as you stay open, aware, and don't run away, you may be surprised by what transpires."

I asked, "If we knew the benefits of things like cover crops as far back as the Roman Empire, why did we abandon them for depleting practices? It doesn't even sound like that much added work."

"Well, I am sure you can look at your society today and imagine why any added steps fell away and why shortcuts became prevalent." After a long pause, he continued, "I love our talks, Mary. I have more hope than I have had for years. My hope in humanity soars when we talk. But my energy is waning, and I believe I need to rest."

"Earlier, you said you were dying. What do you mean by that?"

"I am 155 years old. I have spoken for this set of woods for many years. Another will step up, and I will give my energy to those who need it. It will carry on." I found myself surprised by an anticipated mourning. He must have sensed it, because he said, "Feeling sad for me is so unnecessary. It's the turn of things, and I have served well and existed with great satisfaction."

"In my human world, if we know we are dying, we often have an idea as to when, in months. You?"

"No," he answered, "but I don't believe these roots will feed me for another winter."

"I will let you rest. Should I limit my visits in the future?"

"No, I would love to have as many talks as we can. I feel a bit revived after each visit."

I went to him and wrapped my arms around as much of his trunk as I could. I held the hug. "Till next time."

Chapter 26

IN THE UNCANNY WAY THINGS COME UP WHEN one is in need, I saw a tweet about the Earth Day event happening the next day. I knew there was one every year, but the weather was crap most years. Tomorrow was predicted to be both warm and sunny. Fate wanted me to attend.

I was surprised by the number of vendors, and the good weather drew many people. I saw vendors selling organic foods and promoting gardening, solar heating, and wind energy. Then I saw Portia at a booth selling flowers.

I made a beeline to her booth. "Hi! I didn't think I'd know anyone here."

With a surprised face, she said, "Happy Earth Day, Mary. How's your plant doing? Thriving, I hope!"

In my usual self-deprecating style, I laughed and said, "It's good. Thriving may be overstating it, but I haven't killed it yet."

She looked pleased to see me, and said, "What brings you here?"

"Just trying to be informed, open my mind. I have been learning about soil and the changes in its quality. I thought I might get some literature here."

"I can probably tell you much of what you want to know. My degree is in botany, but there is a scientist down at the other end. He may have some data. If not, come on back and I'd be happy to share my sage information," she said with a wink.

I walked down to the end. The man was at a booth for the International Wildlife Organization. He was dark-haired and his green eyes stood out through his brown blockish glasses. I noticed his olive skin as he was organizing brochures and handouts of articles. I walked up and introduced myself, saying that another vendor had thought he would be able to answer my questions. His face lit up, happy to have someone stop by. I asked him about the science behind soil depletion. One would have thought I offered him a million dollars. It was as if he'd been waiting a lifetime for someone to care about his pet topic.

He picked up an article from the United States Department of Agriculture titled "Natural Resources Conservation Service." He handed it to me, and I glanced at it, knowing I was stepping into a different world. It was a world where he'd quickly know I didn't belong. I saw the words hydric soil and urban soil. There was data packed onto the page. I scanned his booth, pointed to a poster behind him, and said, "I should tell you before my eyes begin to spin in opposite directions from your science-y explanation that I am probably more that poster's speed for soil information." It was a clearly drawn cycle of what transpires under the earth and also clearly intended for the third or fourth grade science text. He smiled a smile which told me he was a little disappointed but still happy to be doing something besides sitting and watching people pass by.

He explained the powerful network of communication and how science is showing that the plants come to each other's aid when they are weak. *I guess that's what Populus Tremulous was referencing that he would still be giving to his community even after dying off. Wow, his real name rolled off my brain.*

I asked him about the urgency of a problem. He indicated there are so many urgent issues that all intertwine, and each person needs to decide their own quest and take that one the direction they find. He explained that his role in IWO is to pull much of the information together and to educate regarding the big picture. No one response can fix it all. He handed me some articles he said discussed what once had single solutions had given way to more complex issues.

Offering his insight, he said, "In my opinion, there are so many factors. We bicker and enact new laws that get rescinded by some later administration. Big business impact and lobbying are hard cases to crack. People are so removed from where their food, and every product, comes from, that we just languish in our enjoyment of easy-made dinners and easily accessed toys."

He gave me his business card. "You look like someone who needs a quest. Feel free to contact me for more information once you decide." I thanked him, but thought, *Why does everyone keep using that word? Quest.*

I looked at the card as I made my way back to Portia's booth. Jason. *He was quite cute in a studious way.* Portia finished up a sale, then asked, "You were gone a while. Did you get some good info, some answers?"

"Yeah, the guy is with the International Wildlife Organization. He was able to dummy down the language so it made sense to me. I got the fifth grade version."

Portia asked, "Mary, what would you think of going for a hike together sometime soon? I don't have enough friends who actually like to get out in nature. You can pick the place."

"Portia, that sounds great." Putting her name in my contacts, I handed her my phone to put in her number, then I texted her so she'd have mine. "I will text you when I know which days I have off the next few weeks and see if you can get away."

●●●

Once I got home, I sat with Tequila on the patio and began scanning the articles. One mentioned how the Cuyahoga River catching on fire in Cleveland, Ohio, during the late 1960s had been a hard thing to ignore. Some simple concrete steps, not requiring much personal sacrifice, went a long way in restoring health to the river's ecosystem. *I remember watching a clip about that in middle school social studies. It led to laws that created the EPA and the Clean Air Act.* It was the same in the 1970s when fluorocarbons in aerosols were banned because they were felt to be influencing a hole in the ozone. *Maybe I knew more than I thought. I had heard of CFCs. My mom had talked about the ripple of momentary panic from women when hairsprays had to change due to the ban of CFCs.* As I read, I began to understand so many interactive parts contributed to the climate issue. People felt overwhelmed, with both life and sorting out this issue. I knew even though I started with good intentions, it had been hard for me to remain devoted to simple recycling when I got too busy. It seemed no one agreed on what one element was most important.

Chapter 27

I WALKED INTO THE WOODS. WHEN I GOT BACK to Cowboy, I placed my mat, sat down, closed my eyes, and visualized talking with him. Nothing happened after an inordinate amount of time. I opened my eyes and was startled when I looked up into the tree. All the other trees had deep green leaves, but Cowboy's branches were bare. I hadn't really noticed they weren't emerging when others were. A level of panic rose in my chest. *Cowboy, do you hear me? Are you ignoring me, maybe done with me?* Nothing.

"He's gone," a woman's voice said. I looked around.

"Who's gone?"

"The one you rudely call Cowboy."

I was not speaking aloud. "Where and who are you?"

"I am deeper in the woods. I am stepping in as guardian of these woods."

"Cowboy died? I know he said he was dyING, I didn't know he meant so soon!"

"Let's henceforth refer to him by his real name, Populus Tremulous."

"I think I need to see your face, where are you exactly?"

"Look a few trees behind Populus Tremulous."

I stood and walked back. I was taken aback. For all the howdy partner friendly look of Cowboy, this tree had on a tough game face. *Game Face*, I thought. Hesitantly, I said, "Uhm, hello."

Apparently seeing my apprehension, she said, "I know Populus informed you how our faces become formed based on what is going on at the time of our seedling. Mine was the Women's Suffrage movement. I know I look stern, and it is true, I don't mess around. Messing around would not have gotten those women anywhere."

A bit irritated, I said, "You sound mad."

"I am not mad but also not as comforting as Populus was. He was a great leader, but we are quickly running out of time. Time for niceties is over. To use a human metaphor, it's time to shit or get off the pot."

I sarcastically said, "I guess you are gruffer. I was still in the fact-finding and exploring part of this quest. I hadn't agreed to take it up."

"Responsibility isn't always an agreed-upon role. Sometimes it's just thrust on us and next thing we know, we are leading the effort, wondering how the hell it happened, exclaiming, 'I didn't sign up for this!'"

"Sounds like you are talking from experience."

"I am an observer. That's merely an observation. Populus and I had been communicating for a long time about this issue of our soil. I wanted to be more aggressive in the approach."

I couldn't help responding, "If I have to say at this very moment, 'Woohoo I accept this quest, yes, I am on board,' then I probably won't come back. If you are willing to keep the dialogue alive, I will be."

Essentially ignoring my statement, she said, "Have you been gathering comrades?"

Somewhat astounded by the term, I repeated, "Gathering comrades?"

"No one can take on an earth issue solo. You need people backing you, along with people at your side, and people who believe even more strongly than you do, so when you wane in endurance, they keep you buoyed. So are there others?"

"I have coincidentally met a couple of interesting women, both who understand soil better than I do. And I met a scientist at the Earth Day fair. Don't know that any are looking for a quest."

"Populus said you are a 'communicator' and are more than you know. My quest may be to get you to believe that. Along that line, stop thinking of it as a grand quest. You are not being sent on a distant journey. We are hoping you can awaken some sleeping minds."

It suddenly washed over me what had transpired. I had this developing friendship with a tree who had a gentle pace, seemed all-knowing and guiding. Now I have this "get-'er-done, game-faced tree.

She continued, "I know you had a good relationship with Populus. You were feeling comfortable in your ambivalence and his allowing for a gradual awareness or even no commitment. I recognize I am coming through with a different urgency. If Populus was more fatherly, think of me as more sisterhood-oriented. I am not one to cater to the low self-esteem. Many people have passed this way over the years. You are only the third human Populus has chosen. He was hoping the third time was a charm."

"He mentioned a first attempt. The second, I happen to know, by the way."

"Yes, there was another before your lifetime. A male. It was too early. Before Earth was showing the outward signs that nature was feeling. I assured him this was a job for the female of your species."

"I agree women get things done, but I will hold onto the 'why me' question until I figure a bit out."

Acquiescing to my pace, she replied, "Obviously I can't chase after you. I can only encourage you to look at your talents and potential."

I asked, "Tell me what you know about the soil depleting? How do you all communicate? How do you know what's happening across the country, let alone in these woods?"

"You are becoming informed about soil depletion. That was not a problem during early practices of farming. The use of compounds such as sulphur were common in ancient times … 4,500 years ago, by a people named the Sumerians. And 3,200 years ago, Chinese peoples were using mercury and arsenic compounds for controlling body lice. It's not new; it's the new level of toxicity that has been reached."

I was listening, so she continued. "The first legislation providing federal authority for regulating pesticides was enacted in 1910; however, decades later during the 1940s, manufacturers began to produce large amounts of synthetic pesticides, and their use became widespread after your World War II. By 1950, pesticides were found to increase farm yield far beyond pre-WWII levels. It was the primary way to combat insects affecting crop yield. When you pair that with other issues such as monocrop planting, leaving fields fallow, and overgrazing ... there comes a critical mass point where the pace of things accelerates, and we are fast approaching the point of no return."

I asked, "Why are they so harmful?"

"Their mode of action is by targeting systems or enzymes in the pests which may be identical or very similar to systems or enzymes in human beings and, therefore, they pose risks to human health and the environment. They are designed to be harmful to something. Sadly, their harmful reach is hard to control. They can have beneficial effects to preserve food, control diseases, and so on. They are now everywhere in the environment simply because they have infiltrated nearly every living thing. Due to our earth's amazing network of self-healing, we who live and survive on and in the soil could withstand most assaults." I found myself thinking, *Maybe even our microbes grow weary.*

I spoke up, saying, "A scientist I met the other day said 2.26 million tons of active-ingredient pesticides were used in 2001. Most were used in agriculture. The most widely used pesticide is herbicide. The use in the US doubled from 1960 to 1980, but has since stabilized or fallen."

"Yes, we are talking about long-term impact. Even as more are transitioning to organic farming, many are not, and there is still much runoff, seepage into the groundwater, spray drift, and so many other ways it travels."

I said, "I have so much to learn. I am starting to believe the importance of this. How do I impact it?"

"How do you, as a human, start to teach anyone about that which they know nothing about? You don't start with hard-to-read graphs and facts and thirty-page research papers. You figure out what they know, and you start there. You motivate them by making it relevant to them. You intuit what they can absorb and what they can emotionally handle. You move from there. In your work of helping people, you make a different-size plan for each person, but your experience makes it easier to know where to start. This isn't as new to you as you are thinking. Use that knowledge in this arena."

"It is hard to wrap my head around the fact that if people know it's harmful, why do they keep manufacturing it, and why do they keep using it?"

"So many things over the centuries started from benevolence, with creative problem-solving and applying one concept to another to solve it. Often good is done. Sometimes harm is done as an unanticipated byproduct, and then there are the times when harm is known, and worse, harm is anticipated but done anyway. That is control and greed personified. A quality special to the human species."

Trying to absorb her information, I said, "I am making connections with this. Like medicines, antibiotics help so many, but if someone is allergic, then it's harmful, so we don't give it to that person anymore. We apply knowledge of another medicine for that person. Medicines help so many and have a benevolent premise. Greed took over in the use of pain meds. Initially, drug companies developed them to help relieve suffering. They knew they were addictive, which is why titrating had to occur to eliminate them. Yet, over-selling them was promoted. That came to light, and it mirrored the tobacco company campaign to addict more people while hiding the impact. So here we have the pesticide-producing companies."

She shifted topics, "Let me move onto your question about communication. How I know what is happening across the woods and then around the earth. Our systems of communications are similar to your development of your nonverbal communication systems. In the 1840s, the telegraph allowed for brief communications through lines of wire across miles and miles using relay stations. It allowed quick delivery of delightful, sad, and troublesome news. There was the pony express in the 1860s, to make letter delivery faster. Then there were telephones and air transportation, making everything faster. Then by 1990, you had the internet."

I jumped in, "There's a prime example of something starting with an exciting and good purpose, then morphing into something of questionable result. Most Americans have a love-hate relationship with the internet."

"We, Nature, have always had your internet. We didn't always have such a need to communicate across the earth, but we could. There are the fungi, the nematodes, mycelium, and all the microorganisms, the connecting fibers beneath. It is how we aid others, how we ask for help, and how good and bad 'nutrients,' along with information, get to us. Our difference is that no one aspect goes rogue for self-preservation or to benefit itself. Your form of currency has historically led to greed in those who cannot be satiated. It is the god too many of your kind worship. We are one and our source and our purpose is each other."

I inhaled to my fullest through my nose, and said, "My head is starting to spin. I am glad I asked the question, yet not so much. I am seeing this is not as complex to understand as it seems, although I know the devil is often in the details. I think class needs to be over for today. Any homework assignments?"

"No. Thanks for listening to me. I know my style is different. Just remain open to messages around this. Time is of the essence."

Chapter 28

I WAS MORE THAN SURPRISED WHEN I GOT TO work the next day. Someone had brought a bunch of plants with a sign above them saying, "Free to caring homes." My one felt like plenty to me, but I thought if any were left by the end of the day, I might rescue a small one as a companion plant.

A bigger surprise laid in store. When I passed Barbara, she asked if I was going to take one of her plant offshoots. I guess she was asking everyone, so it wasn't just me. What surprised me was that she even liked plants and apparently had a nurturing side. I explained I was a plant newbie, and if there was one left at the end of the day, I might.

"You should take one that is more flexible. One you can't do much wrong with. I'd be happy to pick one of those out for you." I nodded my head and hesitantly said, "Okay," as I walked away. I thought, *Who is this woman, and what did they do with the Barbara I had resented so much?*

I had planned to go see Lena during her lunch. When I got back to the wing, the nurse stopped me and said, "You should know that Lena took a turn last night. She's still fairly alert but much weaker."

I entered her room quietly in case she was sleeping. "My hearing is mostly diminished for the lovely bird sounds. I heard your footsteps in the hall."

123

Probably sounding artificially happy, I chimed, "So much for my career as a sleuth. How are ya doing?"

"I got a message last night from the trees," she said.

"The trees?"

"Remember, you aren't the only one in communication with them. My time is near, and except for my time with you, I must say I am quite ready for the next adventure."

"So, what did the trees say to you?"

"Time to feed some other souls. I want a green burial, you know. I have it in a living will. I have told my doctor about it, and the nurse."

"I have heard of it and I'm not completely sure what it means, but I will reinforce your wish when the time comes."

Being a good daughter of the American death and dying culture, I tried to add hope to the situation, thinking maybe she'd recover from … what? Old age?

Assuring me, she spoke gently, "You are viewing this as a sad time. I know you know my age. You have been a bright spot in my days lately, and I am blessed to have gotten to know a person who will be helping the earth as you will."

"Still denying that potential over here," I replied.

Strong enough to roll her eyes, she said, "Don't hold back from who you are becoming. You have been afraid to leap most of your life. You must be growing weary of that story, that story where you aren't enough."

Jokingly, I said, "Your blindness has made your inSIGHT a bit annoying."

"If the shoe fits, truth hurts, hiding in plain sight … They all apply, don't they?" she quipped.

"Yeah, yeah, yeah. Lena, in getting real, I hate that there may be no one here with you when the time comes."

"No one is truly alone, you know. I have so many who have gone before me. I am sure they will gather around. Can't wait to see Harold and my old friends, with my eyes."

Tears filled my eyes as I felt the sadness of losing Cowboy, along with the loss of another who had seen me at a time when I really needed to be seen. Particularly because I didn't know how much I needed it. Others wouldn't understand my grieving for this woman I'd just met a couple months ago. I took her hand with mine and told her I would come back before I left work. She moved her other hand to my arm and stroked it, gliding back and forth over the mole.

"This is feeling a little different. Many things are changing for you. It's okay, Mary, you need to get back to work. Life is a river and it keeps flowing."

As I walked out, the movement of others around me felt surreal. I was walking away from a person, knowing I may never see her again. It wasn't the level of caring. It was the level of peace I was feeling from knowing what we'd meant to each other. She knew how much I cared, present or not. But as I reoriented to the people around me, they had no idea how much my life had changed at that moment. For them, the world was the same as fifteen minutes ago. Mine was forever changed.

The entire day was becoming surreal. First Barbara, then Lena, now Barbara again. I decided I would take a plant in honor of Lena. I hunted down Barbara, "Could you put a sticky note with my name on it by one of the plants that can stare death in the face and scoff? I think that's the one for me."

When I got to the break room, there was a plant with my name by it and a list of suggestions for caring for it. It was written in a lovely script. Barbara had taken time, which surprised me. I wasn't sure which thought path I should go down. Barbara was baiting me for something? Barbara wasn't such a bitch after all? She had a gentler side than I knew? She liked plants more than people? Regardless, they all led to a reminder that what people show us isn't always ALL they are.

I gently raised the plant. *You're coming home with me. I apologize in advance but will do my best in honor of Lena.* I wanted to show it to Lena and tell her it would always remind me of her. Later as I got to her room, I noticed the curtain was pulled around her bed, but I didn't see any other legs from underneath. My heart knew what that meant. Patty, the nurse, approached me. "She just passed about ten minutes ago. The funeral home staff will be here in a half hour or so."

"They know she wants a green burial, right?"

"Yes, her instructions were clear."

"Was anyone with her?"

"I was. I have heard all sorts of final words over the years. 'God told me to get up.' 'Hi Aunt Ginny.' Lena's words were, 'Nice plant.' Maybe she was a gardener?"

I smiled softly and thought how much I was just beginning to see the real world. I only said, "She did love trees."

I asked Patty, "Can I go in and sit a moment?"

She nodded, "Sure."

I entered the room and pulled back the sheet covering her head. I gazed at her for a bit and said, "Your questions, along with recognizing something in me I wasn't seeing, will go with me forever. You must be leaving many legacies of influence, but this is mine." I showed her my plant but said, "However, you apparently already saw it." I placed my hand on her cheek. I stroked it as she had done. I gazed a little longer. "Thank you, Lena. Safe travels." And replaced the sheet, smoothing it over her thinning hair. I left the room and waved an acknowledgment to Patty as I left the wing. Right or wrong, strong or weak, I didn't really want to watch her body be taken away. I watched that with my mother. Once was enough. I'd rather have her leave in my own vision, in a field of light, in a field of wildflowers.

Chapter 29

I HADN'T CRIED AT WORK OR EVEN ON THE way home. The whole prover-bial kid routine of not crying after a fall until you see your mother was true here, except it was my cat, my apartment, where the safety engulfed me. I wasn't sure if I was crying more for Lena or Cowboy, for a human or for a plant. I'm not sure it even mattered. Grief is grief. Still, it felt odd to somehow feel they were on an equal plane of influence and connection.

I drank a beer and cried on the patio, listening to the birds and watching a gray squirrel run a spiral up and down the tree. I took a deep breath followed by one of those releasing audible sighs. *I need to honor their deaths ... should I say shifts in existence. I need more research.*

As I turned on my computer, I found myself thinking about Matt. Person Matt, not Tree Matt. Somehow his arrival seemed to coincide with a series of interesting events. Did his arrival merely coincide? Did he come because I needed awakening? Was his arrival incidental but just the teeny nudge I needed to awaken? If not him, would something else have occurred to initiate the awakening? After a while, I realized the best way to honor Lena and Cowboy was to start trying to understand the nuances of soil.

Chapter 30

I FOUND MYSELF GOOGLING BIOCIDE ENTERPRISES. JUST A BIG conglomerate I'd heard of. I easily discovered it was recently bought by Cura-corp, a company from France. *Funny, I presume a European company is going to be more environmentally sound than an American one. Am sure that's not necessarily true.* Biocide Enterprises shifted from controversial products such as DDT, PCBs to biotechnology.

Next, I searched: big business in agriculture. Most companies I had never heard of, and some sounded more benign like those that made potash. Cargill was still family-owned and known for animal nutrition science. *That sounds kind.* I read something complex about another company that had developed seeds resistant to being harmed by their own pesticides. They knew there was a market in selling these, possibly to farmers who didn't want the pesticide but whose crops were impacted by the spray drift from other farmers. It seems they keep "fixing" the problem by causing more problems and disguising them as helpful to farmers. They may not even know how to unravel their own knot they've created. There was so much data and so much detail, I knew I was way out of my league in judging the efficacy of the information, let alone understanding it.

Note to self: Find the business card for the scientist. What was his name?

... Jason something.

Turned out I didn't need to find the card. I had put my name, cell, and email on a form when I donated ten dollars to the International Wildlife Organization that day. He emailed me. It was a generic email thanking me for my donation but then edged into specifically remembering our meeting and wondering how I was doing on my soil research, offering to answer questions if I had them. *Wonder if everyone gets such personalized responses, or maybe I was one of the few to stop by that day.*

I realized I was getting to the nitty-gritty of this quest. *I don't care if they say it isn't a quest. I looked up the word and it's defined as an arduous search. This is beginning to qualify. I will have to decide what it all means. Its importance.*

I really need to have some fun. Should I call Kelly? Laurie? I took pause at even the thought of those words. *I feel I have shifted so much these past couple of months. I don't dread work as much as I used to, I have had some fun moments with people, and I am sleeping better with less pills. I feel some hope in the future or at least not such dread of each day. I wonder how Dr. Lewis will view it when I see her next.*

Later in the evening, I fell asleep thinking about Lena and Cowboy. I remember from *The Tibetan Book of Living and Dying* that the journey to beyond after a physical death was three human days. There could be confusion for the spirit, and praying for sight and guidance would be helpful to them. So, I prayed for Lena to find her way quickly and smoothly. I wasn't sure what to think about for Cowboy. The whole soul thing was too deep to ponder tonight. I thanked him for his insights and trust and his openness to providing for his forest. I found myself releasing a quick prayer for him also, to nourish many.

As I slept, I dreamed I was sitting on a bench staring at the mole on my arm. It was harder, like a toe callus. I began to pick at the edges. No tugging pain, I was feeling no sensation from it. I chipped away at the callus and peeled it back. I was fascinated. It revealed a divot in my arm about three inches deep. It was green in the hole and I could see a seedling of a tree with one small green leaf growing at the top. I wasn't disgusted or scared. I stared at it until I was startled by some-one approaching behind me.

I woke up, not thinking to take the time to see who was coming. I realized I had to pee. I sat on the toilet, reviewing that dream over and over, visualizing the tree and remembering my fascination versus being grossed out. *Do I really have a tree beneath this mole? Even the der-matologist said nothing came from the scraping and biopsy they did. No one would think to X-ray or MRI a mole. Imagine the sci-fi-ness of it had they done so, and the tech saw a TREE growing.* As I wiped, I pictured the men in hazmat suits running in and whisking my gurney away, a plastic enclosure surrounding me.

It was 4:00 a.m. and I tried to fall back to sleep. It was still over an hour until daylight. I wanted to tell someone about this. Telling a dream was safe; people enjoyed a touch of bizarre. *I'll text Kelly, she's a self-proclaimed insomniac. She likes this kind of shit.*

Text: Hope your phone is on mute in the event you are sleeping; I don't want to wake you. If not, I had a bizarre dream and just want to tell someone about it.

Moments later, my phone rang. She spoke in a whisper, "Good morning. I was wide awake. I'm heading to the other room so as not to wake Rhett. Do tell." I recounted the dream.

Kelly told me, "I am walking to get my book on dreams by some lady. I never think about them too much but like to look up the meaning."

I was surprised, and said, "You have a dream book?"

"Yeah, someone you know gave it to me a long time ago."

I chuckled, "Oh yeah, I forgot about that."

"Tree, tree, page …" she said as I heard her flipping through the in-dex. She read, "Many symbols are archetypal and thus carry a larger-than-life personal meaning.…Jung considered the tree as an archetyp-al symbol of the self and its process of individuation, as represented by growth and branching out. On a personal level, a tree represents our life, especially family life. Branches spreading into the sky repre-sent growth, seeking a higher understanding, while roots can symbol-ize the things buried or unrecognized potential." Then Kelly added, "That all sounds pretty cool. What do you make of it?"

I thought, We all hear, filter, the way we want. Branching out, higher understanding, but unrecognized potential is what I heard the loudest. I said, "I have had a few messages lately about unrecognized potential. The words that have been used are, 'You are more than you know,' so pretty much the same thing."

"That's intriguing, which wise sages have told you this?"

I chose to respond, "Oh, a couple people I have met recently." *I sure can't say a couple of trees told me.*

"The dream is odd enough; something wants you to listen and take heart. Hey by the way, did you ever find out who built that lean-to?"

"Oh yes, a woman named Bella. She lives upstairs. Apparently, she used to be married to a survivalist of sorts, and she learned outdoor survival skills by proxy. So, no one dangerous or ominous. In fact, Matt, the kid we met reading there, is her foster child. You should see her apartment. It has more plants in one place than you would see in the botanical gardens. She even gave me one, then I got another from Barbara, previously known as the 'bitchy nurse' at work."

"Previously known, well that's a change."

"Other things are changing too, Kelly. I feel more energized in life. I still wish I was working somewhere else, but I am not filled with such dread of the day."

"I am so happy to hear that, Mary. I have surely worried about your mental health at different points."

"You, me, and pretty much everyone," I replied.

"I am going to try to go back to sleep. I know Rhett is going to wake up soon, and then no one sleeps when that happens."

With one eyebrow raised, I said, "I am jealous!"

"Yep, still loving it even though every now and then I just want to say, "Ohhhh, let me sleep a few more minutes ...""

Chapter 31

I HAD A SUDDEN BRAINSTORM. I DECIDED TO SEE if I could get Portia and Bella together. I thought I might email scientist Jason and ask him to join. With some open dialogue, I might get a direction I need to go. *Hmmmm. Only Bella knows about the trees, though, what do I do about that? Cross that bridge once I see who will even come.*

I knew there was no going back to sleep. After a bike ride and a shower, I texted Bella and Portia, asked for their emails, and indicated I wanted to propose an idea. It was too much to put into a text, and I didn't know how to begin explaining what I wanted, since I was not one bit sure what it was I would be wanting. Both responded right away, expressing that their curiosity was piqued.

I sent the same basic letter to Portia and Bella separately. I didn't want obligatory responses and they didn't know each other.

Hi Portia (Bella),

Thanks for your quick piqued response. I wanted to ask your thoughts (and maybe a favor) about an issue I have been pondering. I have been reading in some detail about the depletion of our soil and a bit about big corporations that use some practices that aren't helping the situation. I am not sure about next steps but feeling compelled to do something about the issue. Would you be willing to meet at my place for some adult beverages and snacks with possibly a couple other people to help me sort out some paths? I SWEAR I am not selling anything or giving you a pitch to join a network marketing business. Just wanting to get some clarity on it all. If so, maybe May 15?

Thanks, Mary

The one I sent to Jason was a bit more formal. I thanked him for his letter of acknowledgment and asked how serious he was about answering other questions or giving more information. Then I invited him to my gathering. Maybe a little risky, not knowing him at all, but there would be other people, plus Tequila has always been a good judge of people. She never warmed up to my ex. I wish she'd communicated her concerns more clearly at the time. I also figured a scientist doesn't really seem to fit the profile of a serial murderer.

I was surprised to hear back some level of excitement from all of them. Maybe it was the beverages and snacks that grabbed them. So, we were on for the 15th. It gave me a bit of time.

•••

They were all there by six. Jason arrived first. My memory had misjudged his cuteness level. It went from attractive in a studious way to just plain ol' cute. His glasses gave the classic look of the woman librarian with black-rimmed glasses and hair up in a bun, who suddenly takes it down, revealing she is one hot chick.

I was a bit relieved Portia arrived shortly after Jason. Bella brought Matt. Luckily, I had anticipated and welcomed the idea. I had IZZE sodas for him. I had snacks out, served up some wine and beer, and made introductions with statements about how I knew each person. Then I slowed my speaking and said, "You probably wonder why I called you all here. I want to show you this great business opportunity." Breaking into a smile and before they could cringe, I quickly assured them it was a joke. "I have been spending a lot of time in some local woods. I feel like the woods are seeking some help about the soil quality of our planet. I have been reading about the history, the reasons the soil isn't what it used to be." Looking to Jason, I continued, "Jason gave me some articles about agricultural cycles. I have been reading about herbicides and, like so many things, much of what starts out with benevolent intent devolves into covering tracks and problem-solving ways to maintain the profit margins."

"I am sure enjoying the wine, but what are you hoping for from us?" Bella asked.

"Good question. What do I do with this information? What action is needed? I have such a hard time learning something is a problem and then just setting it aside, pretending it isn't that important. I have written legislators so many times pertaining to other issues, but never feel it shifts anything."

Jason asked, "Who are you trying to inform? Who's your audience?"

"Another good question. Climate issues have been brewing for so long. Even though most of us care, baby boomers aren't where I want to start. It's gotten pretty out of hand under their watch. Maybe I need to reach twenty-somethings. They have time, energy, and passion, or at least I did at their age."

Portia chimed in, "Social media gets the biggest acclaim. Blogs, but they're an all-written format. Everyone is watching or listening to podcasts, even YouTube these days."

Matt perked up, and raised his hand like he was in class. Rolling my eyes, I said, "Matt, you don't have to raise your hand. What's your thought?"

"TikTok!"

"I have heard of it. I am not very familiar."

"TikTok is an app where you can watch short videos others made, but it's easy to make your own and share." I noticed Bella Googling it right away. We all gathered around her phone to watch one of the most-viewed videos by Zach King. "That's pretty wild, over 962 million views!" I added.

"Who watches these?"

"I am eleven, and most kids I know with phones do. They say their older sisters and brothers do too."

Jason added, "That seems like an avenue for the tweeners for sure. Maybe YouTube for reaching a broader audience. I have never started a podcast but have certainly listened to them."

Portia added, "Maybe blitzing several platforms and seeing what activity you get."

"Great ideas. Now what the hell do I say?"

"Well, make it more interesting than Sheldon Cooper and Amy Farrah Fowler's *Fun with Flags* show," Bella joked.

In my head, as ideas were firing around the room, I wondered if I should tell the others the truth about the trees. I could see Bella looking at me with the same questioning in her eyes. I decided not to. Before the evening ended, we all exchanged cell numbers and congratulated ourselves on taking a step toward activism. They were open to helping me navigate social media platforms. We set a date to meet at Brookies for a cocktail and further the plan. *Once I start to feel a bit safer, I can broach the tree subject. Right now, it's all about soil.*

Chapter 32

I WENT TO BED, MY BODY HUMMING WITH ANTICIPATION and ideas but also a low-grade fear. I needed to go in early for the breakfast group tomorrow. The upside of that was that I would get to see the patients with Laurie. We always laughed. We still hadn't quite gotten past the visual of the tall, buffed, gorgeous firefighters walking in the back door after we set off the fire alarm; we still fan our faces when it comes up.

I woke up with an overriding sense of dread. I wasn't sure how I slept even though I knew I wasn't really awake. I hadn't woken to this level of dread in some months now. I must have been catastrophizing in my sleep for it to revive at this level. I covered myself with the sheet, breathing to slow my racing heart. *Ugh, I want to call in sick, but that leaves Laurie working with six patients alone. Not manageable, definitely not safe.*

What am I dreading? I asked myself. *Responsibility, the unknown events, unknown responses, added work equals responsibility. I am tired of feeling responsible. Tired of life. Haven't heard those words in my head for a long time. Glad I have an appointment with Dr. Lewis this week. Maybe I shouldn't be weaning off my meds on my own.* I wasn't expecting to be slingshot back to this place so easily. It was ego versus growth. "Stay downtrodden, don't think big. You will fail. Your depression is real. The hope is not. No one will listen," says Ego.

"Go fuck yourself, Ego!" I said aloud as I flung the sheet off and put my feet to the floor.

I let the moisture from the steam fill my lungs, warming the inside while the outside felt the scintillating tap of each bead of water. Each bead was telling me life was moving and it was okay not to know exactly where. At least I was moving.

I was so glad I managed to get my ass out of bed. OTs get to work before almost anyone in the rehab department, and Laurie had gathered the patients the CNAs hadn't gotten to yet. Everyone was at the table when I arrived. "Good morning, Margaret," I said with a more chipper tone than I was truly feeling. The dread had receded, and I was mostly ready to meet this day. The trays came and Laurie was checking to ensure all the adaptive equipment, the items needed for them to eat independently, was with each tray. "Yay! 100 percent today," she said. "I need to stop by and thank the tray preppers. This is a rare success." She kindly quizzed the patients who could explain to see if they could verbalize how things should be set up. She knew 100 percent correctness by busy staff was rare and made self-advocacy paramount.

"I need the spoon put over my left hand to help me scoop by myself."

"I should get mechanical soft fruit."

"I need the sticky stuff under my plate, so it doesn't slide."

Hazel's aphasia still prevented her from free-form expression, but luckily her processing had improved dramatically. I demonstrated a series of silly, unlikely uses of the adaptive equipment, checking to see if she thought I was doing it right. I turned it upside down, put the grip on wrong. Even though she giggled at my antics, "Hungry!" with squinted eyes was her way of saying "Okay, funny, but let's eat already." I heard myself laughing and realized the dread had vanished.

•••

137

I opened a TikTok account when I got home. I saw most uploads were music related. It was a site for short videos, so I had this idea to upload only one fact or piece of information at a time. It should work for our culture's renowned short attention span. One tidbit, one time a day. *People are too busy to read anymore, given their work, kids, and their kids' sports. Nobody wants to come for a face-to-face meeting. Visuals along with the words. Captions ... wonder if I can do captions on TikTok? Gee, with that I should have, oh, I don't know, a week's worth of info.*

I didn't have enough nerve to jump in right at that moment. I needed to decide where to start and realized it would be ideal to have related songs in the background. I could start with Joni Mitchell's *Big Yellow Taxi*, the one about paving paradise. I Googled other songs related to the environment, and realized there were quite a few songs that kids would probably recognize, such as *The Dream Reborn (My President Is Green)* by Markese "Doo Dat" Bryant.

What about YouTube? I thought. *Maybe I need to tag team the message there too. Listen to my thoughts! I am starting, I am doing something. I went from a toe dipped in to considering a dive.*

I got a text from Jason. "I know the A Team is meeting soon, but I'd love to chat before then. Can I call you tomorrow?"

I texted back: "Sure, I am done working at 5, home by 6. Any time after that."

"Til then. Have a good evening."

Hmmmm. Wonder what he's thinking? Time will tell.

As I left work the next day, I thought, *I really want to get back into the woods.* Dare I say, I was being beckoned. I texted Jason and asked if I could reschedule the call to the next night. He texted back a straight-line mouth emoji and a, "Sure. Same time?" I drove a bit farther and, on a whim, texted, "To be honest, I walk through the woods by my house all the time to find my center. That's what has come up. Do you want to join?"

I barely know the guy. My mother's fear-based thinking was questioning the wisdom of going into empty woods with someone I barely knew. *Somehow, we tend to think like-minded people are harmless, yet I know the statistics. Do I even know that much about his thinking?*

He responded, "That sounds great, even better. What time?"

Why's it better? Better to kill me with no witnesses? Shut up, Mom. "Six-thirty will give me time to change and put things in my pack." I calmed my mother's voice by deciding to take my camping knife with me. I knew it was a small token, one that would be little help in a true situation, but it was enough for now.

"See ya then."

He was about as prompt as could be. Pleasantries exchanged, we headed out.

"I don't share this place with too many people. It's close, quiet, and best of all, empty." *Geez, way to give a creep the go-ahead.* I continued, "If word got out, mountain bikers would be next. Nothing against them, it's a cool sport, but changes the energy from peaceful to gonzo." After a pause, "You aren't going to kill me, are you?"

"What?" His face scrunched, eyes widened.

"Never mind. My mom made me ask."

"You talked to your mom about this?"

"No, my mom isn't alive, but her fear-based thinking is alive and well in my head."

"Ah yes, messages from the beyond and long ago that are infused in every cell we have."

"You have them too?"

Changing tones to a deep, authoritative voice, he said, "'You will never make enough money in environmental science to support a family.' So, what do I do? I get an engineering degree, build up lots of student loan debt, and go into environmental work as a low-paid research scientist. I love working for a nonprofit though."

As we passed Matt, I waved. Jason asked, "You wave at trees?" I stopped and said, "Come on back." I walked back a few steps, looked at Matt, looked at Jason, and pointed to the tree. "Tell me what you see." Jason gazed for a moment and his lips grew to a pleasing smile. "Wow. I never would have seen this face without your attention to it."

I urged, "Describe what you see. I am just checking you aren't merely humoring me." He described Matt perfectly. "Good work.

That's only the tip of the iceberg."

I was surprised by his next step. He walked up to the tree and put his hands on the trunk, as a long-lost aunt or uncle might put their hands on your shoulders to gaze at you from just the right distance. Chuckling, I said, "Matt, meet Jason, Jason, Matt." To extend the surprise, he hugged the tree. It wasn't even a particularly short hug. "I can't wait to see the rest of the iceberg."

We walked on. We got to the intersection, and I pointed to Warrior Man. "This one I love. Matt is my welcomer, but maybe this guy is why I feel so safe back here." Jason ran his hand along the bark. He took a step back. "That's one gnarly guy."

"Jason, meet Warrior Man."

"I don't think I will hug him; he looks like that probably isn't his thing."

I affirmed, "He saw a lot through his days."

"You know that becaaausse?"

"A birdie told me. I will show you my favorite resting spot." When we arrived, I said, "Sorry, I only brought one mat to sit on."

"No problem, I like the ground beneath my butt. True grounding through the root chakra."

He scanned the woods, then the sky, for a few minutes. He got up and wandered a bit and came back to sit, scanned a while longer, then leapt up. "You didn't tell me about this one!"

I followed his gaze to Cowboy. This time it was me who smiled. Sharing my friend, having someone else see him, brought me a sense of joy. "I get seeing some faces, probably everyone does that every now and then, kind of like clouds, but THIS! It's a whole person, a persona." He beamed. "Can I take his picture?"

"It's not my woods. I don't think he'd mind. But why?"

I heard a female voice say, "Oh great. The wood's anticipated savior found herself a man. Kiss that quest goodbye." My head jerked up. I looked past Cowboy to Game Face. "You haven't been back in days and now there's this development."

Trying to look nonchalant, unchanging, I said without speaking, "First, there is no development; second, you said it was no quest;

third, I have been quite busy with your charge or whatever it is." The breeze blew, and I sensed Game Face taking a deep inhale.

Calming her tone, she said, "It's true, I have no right for such judgment. My heritage being among the Suffragettes, I saw too many inductees slip away to complacency with a man."

Assuredly, I added, "If history serves me right, some of the most prominent suffragettes were married AND their men were right there with them."

"Touché."

Apparently, I wasn't as nonchalant as I had hoped. Jason asked, "Where are you right now, besides deep in an internal conversation?" He was staring at me, and I said teasingly, "You have missed one."

"One what?"

"Face," I said. "No clues with this one."

"You didn't give me a clue with the last one." Then he said with a challenge in his voice, "Game on."

"Well, you are close."

He began to wander back and forth on the path, looking both ways and looking at each tree. I was envisioning a mechanical eye calculating each inch of each tree. I could tell he wasn't looking deep enough into the woods, only at the front line on each side of the path.

"Okay, one hint, I always sit in this spot." He returned to sit beside me, but continued the calculating rundown of the area, as if measuring it off in quadrants. He shot back up, "This is better than the Where's Waldo or hidden pictures puzzles!" But he wasn't looking at Game Face, he was looking to her left. I followed his gaze and laughed out a "Wah-lah! You found one for sure, but not the one I know. You found your own!" It was farther into the woods, and its pine needles made up part of its personality. It had a kind and knowing look to it.

"Okay Miss Smarty Pants, you tell me what I see."

I said, "A pine tree. A woman with a kind face. A long oval face with a slight point at the chin. A small mouth with thin lips but no nose. Her right eye is made from pine needles that resemble long uplifting eyelashes. From her forehead down to the left side of her upper lip, there are three thick, vertical lines that form a triangle at the top of her lip. These cover where her left eye would be."

"Good description!" he exclaimed.

"I am thrilled you can see them too. Even though I know I am not alone by any means, I have had many people think I am loony." I added, "Before it gets too late, I think I should complete our tour. There's one more place for you to see."

As we walked, I told him it was these woods that made me begin to ponder the soil quality concern. He asked, "But what brought up the soil? Considering the blank stares I get on the topic, I know soil isn't the first thing people think of when they think of climate issues." I hesitated, and left him with, "I was inspired." He responded, "Truly an inspiration since soil is both a key contributing element and one that can alter the tide."

As we entered the clearing, Jason looked around said, "Wow. These woods just keep giving. This place is awesome. Don't tell me you built this!?"

"Ha! No. I thought it might have been built by a scary survivalist when I first discovered it." He interjected, "So your mom really IS in your head, isn't she?"

"Oh yeah, but I found out it was built by my neighbor, Bella actually."

"That's both unexpected and fun." He watched and followed my climbing lead into the blind. The wood bark was warmed by the sun. It was surprisingly comfortable to be so close to him. We sat and peered into the trees from this angle. He suggested, just as a wild idea, maybe instead of a bar, we could all come back here on Friday, explaining it was more fitting for our discussion. He paused briefly, then said, "Uhm, but it's your woods, your gig, I don't mean to be overstepping."

"No actually, it's a great idea. Obviously, Bella has been here, and I'd invited Portia for a hike a couple weeks ago. I am sure we could carry some beers and snacks to suffice."

"Maybe there'd be some woods-inspired thinking. I make a mean margarita. I could make a batch and put it in a cooler backpack."

With a questioning tone, I said, "They make cooler backpacks?"

He laughed and said, "Oh, you have no idea. We are hardly the first to consider drinking in the woods, now are we?"

It became apparent the sun was beginning to lower. "I suppose we should head out. I didn't bring my headlamp."

We downclimbed. My movement was smoother since I'd done it a handful of times, but he was quite agile. I asked, "Do you climb? Downclimbing is a skill all its own."

"I used to but haven't in a long time. Crags got busy, climbing partners moved. Other things came up." We started heading out. He patted Warrior Man, and slapped Matt in that Captain Kirk way, "Good job Matt, keeping watch over the entrance." I smiled and gave him a look that said, "You may not be dangerous, but you have some crazy in you."

• • •

When we got back to the apartment parking lot, Jason stopped by his car, took a deep inhale, and raised his arms above his head. "I feel so relaxed, what a gift to have this place so close." It felt a bit uncomfortable about how to say goodbye, but I said, "It was very fun to show it to someone, and the wood spirits like you well enough to expose one of their own to you."

"Very metaphysical of you, Mary. I will gladly accept the compliment."

"I will text Portia and Bella about the possible change of venue and let you know if Friday in the Woods is a go. Either way, I will see you Friday." I started to walk away, and he called out, "Hey Mary." I turned. "I know I came under a different premise, but this was a serendipitous turn of events. Let's save that discussion for another time."

"Sure, no worries. It was perfect."

I got up to the apartment, rubbed Tequila's head and butt, and walked over to my plants. I smiled and said, "Serendipitous turn of events, indeed."

I realized I hadn't even eaten. I sat down at the computer and munched on some popcorn. The dinner of champions, in my book. I had a little time before going to bed. I wanted to look up an explanation for the current condition of our soil. Something understandable for the adolescent but adequate for the twenty-somethings. I didn't get very far when I remembered I was supposed to text Portia and Bella.

"Hey Bella, what would you think of having a group meeting back at the lean-to versus at a bar?"

Quick response: "Sure, fine by me. Weather looks to be great. Think Jason will be okay with that?"

"Uhm, it was his idea."

Equally quick response: "Oh!? That's intriguing. I think there's more to this story."

"I will get back to you one way or the other."

Next text: "Hi Portia, this is Mary. I know a couple weeks back, I asked you to hike in the woods with me. What would you think if we held our group meeting at this clearing in there? It's pretty cool. No obligation if it doesn't feel right."

Ten minutes later: "We aren't going to dance naked around a fire or anything are we?"

I texted: "Ha! My body image is hardly good enough for anything like that!"

Immediate response: "I am there with ya on that! Sounds fine Mary. Can I come to your apartment first?"

"Yes, that'd be perfect, we can walk together. I will let you know for sure, soon."

Chapter 33

W HEN I GOT INTO WORK, LAURIE DASHED UP to me, saying, "Hey I have been seeing your postings on TikTok! What have you been up to lately? Have you noticed how many viewers you are getting?"

"Me? Mine? Really?"

"They are intriguing. I have obviously been missing out on something important transpiring with you."

"What do you think of them? Am I making sense?"

"Yeah! I really like that you are giving websites at the end which people can go to for in-depth reading. Not that I have done that since I am knee deep in the 'just tell me, don't make me read it myself' mentality. Plus, I trust you."

"I feel honored you are liking it. I have been kind of afraid to watch them after the first couple. I am so self-critical, I'd probably take them down. How'd you discover them?"

"My daughter is all about TikTok and actually recognized your face. She was like, 'Hey Mom, isn't this Mary?"

"Uhm, how many views?"

"It's going up with each of your posts. Probably two thousand or so."

"Oooh, that's surprising and scary. I did look at it the first day and there'd been three views. I figured it was the three people who are helping me with this project. Now I am feeling kind of heavy with responsibility."

Barbara was documenting at the nurse's station and overheard us talking. "What is TikTok and what else are you doing?" she asked.

Laurie jumped in, explaining TikTok and excitedly adding, "Mary's been posting information about the demise of our soil quality and its impact on climate."

"Climate? Really? I may need to figure it out. Are you on Facebook or YouTube with it? I know those."

"Not right now. I have thought about YouTube. I am pretty over Facebook."

Barbara said, "It may surprise you, but I am in an online group that discusses climate issues. Soil doesn't come up much."

Barbara and I have more in common than I thought. I replied, "If you find my posts, let me know what you think." I walked away, noticing an absence of resentment for the woman. I was surprised.

A couple weeks later, I got an invite to join an online group named Medical Workers for the Climate. It was just a link, and I didn't recognize the obscure name of the sender it came from. I decided to let it go. Who knows who was trying to suck me in.

Soon after, Barbara approached me and said, "Hey I sent you a link to the group's meetings."

"Oh, I did get something but didn't recognize the sender so didn't want to get trolled. That was you?"

"Yeah, the administrators of the group have looked at your videos and like the direction you are going with them."

"Who's in this group, anyway?" I asked.

"The administrators are PhDs or MDs who have watched changes in health patterns they believe are linked to air quality and the food chain. Members are from all fields, but most are health care based."

"Would you feel comfortable copying and sending me a couple of their own posts? We all get so inundated once we join something, I always try to know what I am joining. Un-joining never seems very easy even though it says, 'unsubscribe here.'" I filtered out some of the truth in my statement, which was, *I may not hate you*

anymore, but that doesn't mean I am completely trusting you either.
Sounding interested to please, she said, "Yeah, I could do that."

●●●

Later, sitting at home, I heard a knock at my door. It was such a
rare event that I felt suspicious. One would think it'd be a feeling of
excitement since I knew people couldn't solicit here. When I opened
it, it was Matt.

"Hi Matt. This is a nice surprise. Come on in." Matt beelined to
Tequila, and she immediately purred. Cats sense a good soul.

"She likes you. I'm sure she gets very bored with just me. I rarely
take trips but if I do, I'd pay you to come feed and love on her a bit."

"I like cats, and I like money … especially after I took that limo
ride. I want to be rich someday."

"Doing well in school can help that dream come true. But having a
good heart and kind soul are already making you rich, in my mind. I
learned that even when you get those things you thought would make
you rich, the carrot moves."

"What carrot?"

"It's a figure of speech, meaning it's hard not to just want more
once you get those things you thought would feel so good. The prize
ahead of you, the carrot, moves. The point is that happiness really
comes from inside. Can't deny some very, very nice things are wonderful to have, too, and money does make parts of life easier to cope
with." *Odd to hear myself telling someone else about happiness.*

It was obvious I was losing him with my espoused wisdom, "So
yeah, what can I do for ya?"

"Bella Mom said it was okay to come down and let you know some
of my friends are following you on TikTok."

"Well, one, the word friends warms my heart. And two, I wonder
how they found it …"

He said, "One, I moved up the friend chain after the limo ride,
apparently, and two, I showed one person and it went from there."

"The developments are both exciting and scary. It's one thing to have adults invite me to groups, it feels heavier or riskier to have children, should I say, impressionable young adults, watching my posts."

Cocking his head sideways, then pointing to my TV, "Did you ever watch, *Are You Smarter than a 5th Grader*? We aren't fooled as easily as most believe."

"I have little recall of fifth grade beyond a few poems I wrote, boys I liked, and girl drama. Maybe times have changed."

"Girl drama is unchanged. We do see and know much more about the world compared to the old days. ... not that you are that old."

"Ouch, but real. So, what are your friends saying about the posts?"

"They asked Mrs. Smith if it can be shown during the weekly news broadcast. She said climate change topics are considered controversial since not all people accept the concept, but she said she'd look into slipping some in during the Changing Earth unit coming up in science. I do think she's following you now."

"Thank you so much for letting me know. Wow! I am reaching kids your age! You are the ones who can change the world! I really appreciate you giving me the TikTok idea, and joining in on this, Matt. We will have to brainstorm how we can reach other kids your age."

Seizing his "in," Matt said, "I have already been thinking about that. Our school system is huge. A friend has a sister taking environmental science at the high school. Maybe those kids could watch it in class. I will ask him to show it to her."

I had to admit, I did like the idea of older kids seeing it. "Thanks. I owe you a marketing fee! First magazines, which, by the way, I love mine. Then video marketing. You may have a future, Matt." I could tell he knew it was a lighthearted comment, but he still looked pleased. Maybe he wasn't used to encouraging remarks prior to staying with Bella.

"I'd take ice cream as my fee," he said, smiling.

"That's a fee I can afford."

Chapter 34

I GOT BARBARA'S LINKS AND READ THE ARTICLES, AND immediately joined. *The more facts I can access, the better.* Things were starting to happen. I doubted others would describe it as large-scale, but this was certainly further than I had ever gotten in the art of persuasion. I had never felt like my voice was out front. I was the supporter. I can remember working in groups in school and suggesting an idea, getting no response, and then another in the group would repeat my idea, and everyone would jump on it. *It may be time to let some of that shit-thinking go.*

I got an email from the teacher at the high school, asking permission to use my videos.

Hi Mary,

I am the teacher of Environmental Sciences at West High School. I have watched your TikTok videos because a few of my students keep mentioning them, citing information from them. I like that you cite your sources at the end of each one. I wanted to ask if it's okay that I use them in my class.

Sincerely,

Kerri Smith

I was flattered, excited, and actually pretty damn impressed with myself. A post would loop on-screen while students were walking into class, and they would post a comment in the "warm-up notebook. My heart raced. I wasn't sure if it was all excitement or partially fear about where this was really going. That ol' responsibility fear was rearing its head. What would people start expecting of me? Oh yes, there was definitely some of that creeping in to dampen my excitement. It was that voice, the critic that reminded me that I wasn't good enough to go big in the room. It told me to sit back down. *At least I am now aware of that critic so I can keep telling it to sit his own self down. I have stood up to my critic a couple times now. Things ARE happening inside and out.*

I thanked Mrs. Smith for reaching out and said I was excited she felt the videos were useful and to please use them. I requested that at some point, she let me know what kind of comments her students were writing.

Chapter 35

Portia got to my apartment, and we waited for Jason to pull in, then we headed back to the lean-to. Bella had gone in earlier, saying she wanted to check on the tree platform. I didn't tell her it amply held Jason and me not too long ago.

Jason was carrying an interesting backpack. It was rectangular and stuck out about eighteen inches from his back. Essentially, a beer cooler with shoulder straps. "I brought the margaritas. I heard the mix from Costco was incredible. I threw in some water ... don't worry, not plastic, it's Boxed Water. I wanted us to be able to find our way out of the woods."

Portia had some homemade salsa and tortilla chips. She'd made homemade pretzels, too, saying, "Enough salt is key, or else they just taste like dough."

When we entered the clearing, we heard, "Hello dowwwwnnn there." Looking up, we saw Bella lounging, looking down at us with a smile that said, "I fucking love it out here!" Matt was up there, too, hanging dangerously over the edge.

As they both scrambled down with ease, we saw Matt had brought a little bouquet of flowers. We all settled onto the blankets I placed on the ground. Bella had brought some IZZE-like lemonades and handed one to Matt.

"BPA-free plastic glasses," Jason exclaimed as he handed us each our first margarita.

"You even added salt to the rim!" I said. "I love that we are meeting back here. I think the trees will like hearing us talk about their well-being. Let's toast to new friends!" Our plastic glasses made a clunk. Not as rewarding as the clink of glass, but bonding, nonetheless.

Jason said, "I like that we are five versus just four. Matt, you are the future of our world. I am pleased you have an interest in hanging out with us old farts." Matt looked at Jason and laughed. "You aren't old. Old is fifty," to which Jason responded, "Well that's a relief. I have some years before it's over."

We snacked and chatted a bit. I loved hearing Matt share what was happening in school. Even with all he's probably been through, he had such enthusiasm for learning.

Portia asked me if I'd read anything new on the state of the soil. I said I would soon need fresh material for TikTok. Jason offered to make sense of some studies and pare them down to facts people would be able to carry away. We discussed whether I should be the one presenting, or all of us, or two of us ... and we agreed I would do it independently and all names would be added to the credits, except Matt's for child privacy rights.

Looking up into the branches, Bella asked us if we had ever wondered where our souls come from or how they entered our sentient forms. Surprisingly, each of us had considered it. Bella told us her soul was made of meadow flowers. I thought that was beautifully colorful. I said, "I came in the form of a slowly spinning white swirl of energy." Portia said, "I am able to connect to the meadow flowers. I arose from the earth as a series of roots growing into an ethereal tree form."

"Mine is not as beautiful as all of yours," Jason said, adding, "I arose from beneath the ground with nematodes, the microscopic fibers rising and entwining, forming my soul."

"Oh my God, Jason, that is so fitting. You had commented about grounding by sitting on the dirt without any blankets to rest on," I said.

We glanced at Matt, more out of not wanting to exclude him because he was a kid than expecting him to have given this any thought. Jumping at the implied invite, he said, "I don't know about a soul, or about my start. My first childhood memory is hiding in a park with my mom. I don't know what we were hiding from, but she held me close and told me a story of a living woods with trees that name their seedlings after human friends. She said a tree would be proud to have my name, Matt.

We all just stared with admiration for this boy. "Wow," was the inadequate word my mind conjured as it zipped to my vision of my tree sentry, Matt. Portia finally responded, not knowing the whole situation. "Your mom has a very creative mind and surely loves and honors you." I could only imagine Matt's mind was trying to reconcile that mom with his current mom.

Bella decided it was fitting to shift to the billion-dollar question, "Do you think you should tell the others why you broke into this arena and the events that spurred all this?" I looked at her and said, "They might run and leave this loony one in the woods."

Eyebrows went up in both Portia and Jason. Matt said with a strange "knowing" look, "Well, there's no going back on this one, Mary."

"Nope," chimed in Jason.

I sat there looking around the woods, starting to speak, and stopping. Then I blurted, "The trees are talking to me. There, now you can run."

Jason slowly said, "I wasn't expecting that." Portia agreed, "Nor was I. Can't wait to hear you elaborate."

I blew out a big sigh. "Not sure where to start. I have always seen faces in trees. Many people do, even though I don't know many others who do. Not every tree has a face, but they are very apparent to me when they do. They become familiar, almost comforting. One day, one of them spoke back. Naturally, I didn't think it was a tree talking when I first heard it. I thought someone was hiding, watching me in the woods. I actually thought it was the person who had built this place. I stayed away, then went back with another friend. I finally went back to the initial spot and he spoke again. I know it sounds freaky, crazy."

I looked at Jason and said, "It was the Cowboy tree." Both Portia and Bella looked from him to me, and now their eyebrows raised.

Bella joined, "In fairness to Mary, you should know she's not alone. I, too, heard it a couple years back but WAS so freaked out I didn't go back to that spot. But I know I heard something."

Matt said with wisdom beyond his years, blending science and cinema, "Nature is as alive as we are. Remember the Ents in *Lord of the Rings*? Even trees in *The Wizard of Oz* talk."

"I got into botany, horticulture, because I believe in the life force of plants. Can't say they have ever talked to me, but I can say I sense what they need sometimes. I don't know where else the desire to water them, prune them, and move them comes from, except I just feel they need it."

I looked at Jason, "Soooooo, care to weigh in?"

"Y'all are making sense. I believe nature is alive. I don't feel the need to go running from this, but I might do a search of studies about plant intercommunication. We do know that plants communicate with each other in ways we are only beginning to understand. Still, it falls into the slightly bizarre realm but not batshit crazy, if that helps."

"It is somewhat helpful, I suppose," I said.

"Let me ask another question," Jason said. "Did the tree speak out loud or did you hear it with your mind?"

"I heard it with my mind. I sometimes spoke with my voice, but I didn't need to. To add to the oddity of it all, the other day when we were sitting by Cowboy, who, by the way, recently died, his appointed follower was talking to me."

"So, there's more of them?"

"Two, only two, that I know. Many faces, but only two have talked to me. Maybe it's more accurate to say communicated with me. Now that I think about it, I have sensed changes of expression or emotion from the others."

Bella reaffirmed, "I can only tell you what she says is true. I thought I was the crazy one until Mary came to me with this."

Reassuringly, Matt added, "Well I think it's really cool, considering what we didn't know about things back in the old days, the 1960s and 1970s, that we know now. Computers talk to us and we don't think anything of that anymore."

"Hmmmph," I said. "That last tidbit might make me feel saner than I have felt in weeks. Thanks for that, Matt! I will keep going with TikTok, see where that goes. How else should I, we I hope, start telling the world about the condition of our soil and how we can repair it?"

Jason shook his head. "I do know saying trees are talking to you is NOT a good place to start."

"Oh please!" I laughed, "I do know that much."

We laid out a few other ideas, but spent more time enjoying margaritas and telling each other more ourselves. Turns out everyone had been married. Portia surprisingly had a young adult daughter, Jason's ex-wife came out as a lesbian, but he affirmed she's happier than he'd ever seen her and they are good friends. I guess people don't often get out of their thirties without some trauma or an interesting story. Jason was definitely looking at me a lot, and if I didn't know any better, I'd say Bella and Portia were looking at each other a lot too. Matt, well, he just looked like he'd heard this and more in his young life.

One idea we did come up with was for Jason to reach out to farmers who already use soil regenerative farming techniques and see what got them interested in their practice. If it works on a small scale, maybe there's more that can be done on a larger scale.

We found our way out of the woods, despite the margaritas, thanks to the water that Jason thought to bring. Bella and I bid Jason and Portia goodnight at their cars and headed to our apartments. Within a couple minutes, there was a knock at my door. *This knocking is getting to be a regular occurrence!* I opened the door to see Bella leaning against the opposite wall.

"Okay girl, I caught a couple of exchanged glances between you and Jason and noted you had been to Cowboy with him. Is there a little something developing?"

"Ha! I saw your eyebrows raise at that comment. Come on in for a minute. I really am not sure." I explained our text string and that whatever he wanted to say got postponed. I added I was becoming happier on my own than I'd been for a long time and wasn't sure I wanted anything like a relationship to mess that up. "No one says it has to be anything, and besides, he could want to confide about someone else," I reasoned.

Jerking her head sideways, she said, "Based on the way he looked at you, I truly doubt that. Point is to wait until there's something to decide. I was just being nosy and wanted to see if my suspicions were warranted. I told Matt I'd be back in a few minutes, so I will catch you soon." As I shut the door, I thought, *It continues to get interesting.*

Chapter 36

I WAS A BIT SUSPICIOUS WHEN I GOT AN email from an unknown person with a subject line of Project Drawdown. I had briefly seen the name in my research but was still worried it was phishing. I had definitely learned that I couldn't judge a tree by it's exterior. I decided to apply the same to this email. A woman named Lily Ekels had a child who had seen the videos and shown them to her. She lived in the San Francisco area and follows Project Drawdown. She suggested I mention them.

Damn, kids are so aware these days; they are a great way to start a movement. Being the first request, I had gotten, I decided to research the company online before responding.

Project Drawdown seemed to be a legit nonprofit working in the climate solutions space. "Drawdown" referred to "the future point in time when levels of greenhouse gases in the atmosphere would stop climbing and start to steadily decline." In the past couple of years, the organization had emerged as a leading resource for information and insight to help solve the climate crisis. I saw a lot of information about their efforts to partner and collaborate with others to "move the world toward "drawdown" as quickly and safely as possible". They offered the Drawdown Learn Conference and many other opportunities to integrate the ideas and discussions in the teaching and learning communities, and beyond. My head was spinning with the knowledge and opportunities this organization had to offer.

I wanted to get Jason's take on them too. A person can put anything they want on the internet. It could be big business, sucking in misinformed people.

I texted him: "Ever hear of Drawdown, or Project Drawdown? I found it on the internet but seeking backup that they are a real nonprofit, and that they are who they say they are."

Receiving an immediate response. *Geez that was quick* … "Yeah, they are authentic. They seem to be respected within the conservation community. Why?"

I texted back: "I got an email from a woman living in San Francisco, their headquarters are there. She suggested I list them in one of my TikTok videos.

"That is very interesting. How did she get your name?"

"Apparently, the woman who emailed me has a child who had shown her the videos!!"

Jason texted, "Your attention base has begun to span the country!"

"In 15 minutes, I have flipped between excited and scared about 100 times."

"I can tell you that from my knowledge, they are authentic, respected by others."

I texted: "I think I will sit on it for a day. Need to explore how big I want to go."

"You are right. No need to respond immediately, we just feel like there is."

I sat for a moment with all the serendipitous events that had occurred over the past months. First meeting Bella and Portia, then Portia steered me to Jason. Then came all the student enthusiasm, and now this. I had to give credit to Matt. He was the reason I met Bella, got my plant, and met Portia. I scooped up Tequila and slowly stroked her fur as she purred, and I said to her, "Quite the interesting web of events, isn't it?" I realized my deep sadness that had prevailed over my life these past couple of years was receding. I would have liked to say it was gone, but I knew it lurked. Maybe I was finding a new purpose. I wasn't just an ex-wife feeling unworthy, or a speech pathologist tired of the work pace. I was a communicator with a message. I had a deeper calling than I knew.

I jotted down a list of groups that were watching me. "Paying attention" may be a better description.

Students on TikTok, Barbara's environmental group, now adults from farther reaches of the country ... *Hmmm ... do I just wait for others to notice or do I seek it? Do I want to be noticed?*

The answer to that question came the next day, again in the form of an email. It was from Agricorp. I wasn't sure if I felt more excitement or dread. It was an emotion that came with disbelief that I was on their radar at all.

Dear Miss Keeley,

Your TikTok videos have come to our attention. While we understand the points you are trying to make, we also have concern that they are implicating us in mismanagement of the soil. We have been receiving a number of questions from school-aged children who are asking about our practices. We refer specifically to your video titled, Big Business, in which you placed our name first on your list of agribusinesses. We would like to see a video in which you also highlight the good we provide by feeding the masses around the world through our production practices.

Sincerely,

Daniel Meyers,

Communications Director, Agricorp

I got that feeling in the pit of my stomach like the one spurred by the reaction of a patient's family, and my brain would shoot to scenarios involving a lawsuit, an ethics committee, and ending up with me going to jail. Logically, I knew I had done nothing wrong and had made sound choices, but the fear-based part of my psyche leapfrogged to the forefront and captured my frontal lobe, silencing any logic, and I only could see myself in a cell wearing orange.

I texted the group: "I can't believe what I just got ... an email from

Agricorp. I am going to copy it in another text. It's got me kind of freaking out."

I heard back first from Portia: "I saw that video they reference. You didn't imply anything negative about them. You merely named them. I wouldn't worry, let alone freak out."

Then Bella: "I agree with Portia. If students thought to write them, they were using the skill of inferencing and taking the next step on their own. You didn't say, 'Write them because they have bad practices' or call out anything specific."

Later that day, Jason weighed in: "Ah yes, first line of defense. Presume the person will be easily called off. Will you be, Mary? Agree with above texts. Nothing to stand on, yet. Might be time to post the good, the bad, the ugly video. That'd be responding to the 'please post the good we are doing' request." He added a smiley face.

I felt better but also found myself thinking I needed to step up my research. Being a speech pathologist and someone who always worried about the impending, albeit, unlikely lawsuit, I had found that preparation was key for my mental health.

I knew that Curacorp had recently acquired Biocide Enterprises, so I checked out the Curacorp website and found their perspectives on soil issues. Their site like others I'd read, shared details about the complexity of the soil, the time it takes to form small amounts of surface soil, and the billions of microorganisms it hosts. I kept reading, and could see that they were aiming to share their expertise in soil and agriculture. In other Googling I came across a quote of the Food and Agriculture Organization of the United Nations: "Despite the huge relevance of soil, the conditions of the available land on our planet are worrisome. More than half the world's agricultural land is moderately to severely degraded with 12 million hectares lost each year"

It sounded like some companies GET it. But did they? Why did I feel so suspicious that the big companies truly had a magnanimous, benevolent intent? Probably some employees did, but I imagined they got sucked up, pushed out, sidelined, or minimized in favor of the profit lines and CEO salaries. It felt like it was smoke and mirrors to stop me from easily finding information about practices, such as when a company, instead of stopping the spraying of a detrimental product, re-engineered their seeds to grow and be resistant to what is being sprayed. I thought about what most people eat and wondered how many degrees of separation those products are from the original seeds created by nature.

Chapter 37

I WASN'T SURE WHAT TO DO NEXT, AND IT occurred to me I needed to go where I always find peace—to my trees, my woods. Grabbing only my pad and some water, I saw little along the way. Later, I wondered if Matt and Warrior Man felt dismissed. After all, they were the ones who stood sentry and guided me further into this story I was living.

I sat in front of Cowboy. I felt a sadness that his gentle, knowing, and understanding voice was silent. Did he know it might require a different catalyst for action? I looked at Game Face. *God, I really need to come up with better names. It's almost demeaning, like calling a beloved dog, Dog. Populus Tremulous, not Cowboy.* Not feeling very capable in the naming realm, I turned my head to Game Face and asked her what she'd like to be called. As if she was relieved I had finally bothered to ask, she said, "I have always liked the name Emmiline. Emmiline Parkhurst was a British suffragette inspiring many in the Americas movement."

"It does sound beautiful. Alright, Emmiline, I am actually having some fun igniting young minds about the soil's great need, but I worry I have also caught the Eye of Sauron while moving through this. I am not much of a warrior. More of an avoider."

"That reference, I don't really know."

"Eh, it's from a current classic. It implies someone is watching you that you don't want to be noticed by."

She said, "Close your eyes for a moment. Just breathe. Feel the ground beneath you. Listen to its message." I was sure I felt a warming from more than just my butt having been there awhile. This warm energy began to spiral around my hips up to my waist, swirling onward to my shoulders. "This is very comforting," I said.

"The earth is always here for you. The mycelium communicate how you are doing in your not-a-quest. We are appreciative and will help you regenerate when you feel alone. Your friends are there for you to lean on. Remember, you do not need to go this alone."

I opened my eyes and Emmiline's needles were shimmering as they do when clinging raindrops shimmer in the sun. It hadn't rained. The leaves of the aspens around her were gently swaying even though there was no breeze. "We all appreciate and applaud your willingness to help."

"Thank you, Emmiline." I smirked and added, "You are more than I initially judged."

"Aren't we all," she replied.

Feeling renewed, I walked back as I considered all I had just witnessed. As I approached the fork, I looked up to see Jason resting on Warrior Man.

"I am not stalking you. I saw Bella and Portia as I was walking to your apartment. Bella said Matt had seen you walk toward the woods. I didn't know which route you took so thought I'd wait here, knowing you'd eventually pass by. I was having a chat with Warrior here, when I saw a swaying of the aspens and a shimmering of the pines without any breeze. Did you have anything to do with that?" He stood as I approached.

"I was a recipient of it, not an instigator. Wasn't it lovely?"

"It was." He gently but solidly put his hands on my shoulders as I leaned back against the tree. "As are you, Mary. You are one of the loveliest, most unassuming people I have met in many years. It is what I wanted to tell you that first time I came to your apartment. I couldn't wait to say it any longer." One hand touched my cheek, and he kissed me and pulled back to check how it was received. I felt a pulsing rush I hadn't felt in years. Looking into his eyes and putting my hand behind his neck, I pulled him toward me, placing my lips on his cheek, then kissing his lips. I couldn't be sure how long we held the luxurious warm connection, but I definitely was looking for more. "I have an idea," I said, taking his hand and choosing the path to the lean-to. We didn't speak in the few minutes it took to get there; both of us were aware of our silent agreement.

As we stood embracing, he slid to the forest floor and laid back, guided me down onto him. *Oh my God, nothing like only thin material between us, to wake up every dormant cell!* It felt slow and sweet with urgency. I'd never had sex anywhere interesting and felt a thrill knowing, as I was kissing this man, that I could likely kiss that fact goodbye. He rolled over, placing me on the earth underneath him.

"My Lady of the Woods. Let's see what else we can make shimmer." He looked directly into my eyes, gently placed his hands on my hips and I felt him slowly gliding down. *God, I hope he's decent at this.* He knew exactly where to kiss, how to blow a warm breath of air on just the right spot, what to whisper, and definitely where to linger. *Oh, yes. He knew what he was doing.* I heard myself gasp, while I felt my body arch up in an intensity that ushered in a wave. I closed my eyes at the pleasure and felt electricity coursing through my body.

Eventually, I turned my gaze back to him and saw that he had an accomplished smile. He started sliding my clothes back into place.

"Wait, don't you want ...?"

He sprang to his feet from the forest floor, grabbed my hand, and helped me up, saying, "Let's just say I am hoping we will do more of that in the future. For now, I can say I'd been thinking of your beauty since you showed up at my booth on Earth Day. This interlude was not what I had envisioned as I waited by Warrior Man. The woods inspired me." We laughed and held each other for a moment, enjoying our cleansing breaths that seemed to be in sync. We made our way out of the woods to his car.

"Oh, now that I am thinking clearer ... you saw Bella AND Portia? Together? This morning?"

He nodded, raising his arms in a "who knows" gesture.

He kissed my forehead, "I need to get some work done. Much more likely to concentrate now."

Chapter 38

BACK IN MY APARTMENT, I FELT A LIGHTNESS. Part of me just wanted to roll with what had transpired. Part of me was chastising myself for relating my "lightness," my happiness, to something a man had done. I'd come to loathe the feeling that I needed a man in my life. *It was one interlude, Mary. Don't get ahead of yourself. Having had sex isn't the same as needing someone in order to be happy.* To change my head's direction, I decided to email the communications director back. I had written a thousand reports and many letters to families over the years. I had documented sensitive information. I could handle this.

Mr. Meyers,

Thanks for reaching out to me with your concerns. I have to admit it's exciting students are reaching out to you and asking questions. I hope you, too, see it as a positive sign of young people taking on civic duties of expressing concerns. I didn't implicate Agricorp in anything but it does seem reasonable that I can run a series of something positive each company is developing in order to balance any questioning I may pose. Since you have reached out, I am sure you have some efforts in mind you would like me to put forth. Feel free to send information my way and I will review and research them.

Sincerely,

Mary Keeley

•••

I hadn't done much with the third eye concept lately. I decided to sit and focus, even though the sun wasn't setting. I found myself re-envisioning my dream about my mole and what I saw in my dream. As I peered into the space, I discovered the seedling with a leaf now had two leaves. I thought of the cells that make up our skin, the veins that course through our bodies, the cilia in our inner ear, the brain's neural pathways, and all the unique parts of the information highway that make up our bodies. The soil holds many of the same fiber networks. We know that when any one part of our body's network breaks down, illness or impairment sets in somewhere. Yet we are so quick to dismiss the same impact of interconnectedness within the earth.

I think the next few postings will be about people or companies who are doing good things. I have gone through some facts. Now name some companies, shout outs, so to speak. I would start with Project Drawdown since there had been a specific request.

Our group started calling ourselves the ModQuad ... a play on words for the 1960s TV show, *Mod Squad*. None of us were alive when it was on, but my mom used to talk about spy shows that were popular in those days. We were kind of like spies for the earth.

It was unspoken but apparent among each in the group that relationships were evolving with Jason and me, and with Bella and Portia. The energy was keeping the enthusiasm level high with a continual air of celebration.

After my post, I got another email from Lily Ekels. She'd seen a blurb in a local paper indicating Project Drawdown had seen a spike in donations. This told me other people were paying attention, not only the students, if money was being donated. My hits for the videos were rising every day, and I was getting way more shares than I had at first. I realized how little I knew about the world I had stepped into. It made me excited and reticent. Was I stepping into something too big? Could I get in trouble? Sometimes I wondered what happened in a previous life, or what happened when I was young, that gave me this submerged but strong sense of foreboding anytime I stepped out and raised my voice. *I have been hiding in plain sight so much of my life. I am sick of that fear-based thought pattern. I know I worry that people won't notice, so sometimes I don't do something because then there's no chance I could be ignored. Their possible rejection of my ideas gets interpreted as a rejection of me. Crap, then on the flip side, I fear succeeding and having people expect more of me.* I knew it was a conglomerate rock of both of these emotions, and I was D.O.N.E.!

Chapter 39

People who knew what was happening began asking me why I took on this task. They wondered what got me involved. Yeah, they knew I'd always liked hiking and the outdoors, I was a recycler, and I bought mostly organic, but this was a completely different level of activism. Instead of personal choice action, this was promoting a specific aspect to impact climate change. Joining in behind the scenes had always been my preferred method, and people close to me knew that instigating, leading, was not my way. I was a terrible liar, so I typically stumbled around but settled on the story of seeing an article that spurred my interest. I kept asking myself what would happen if I said the trees had talked to me. Talk about opening doors for ridicule. Yet I knew there were many people out there who would also treasure such a thought, embrace it, feel liberated, and run to the woods in hopes of hearing their own set of voices.

I began by sharing quotes, such as those by Native Americans.

From the Arapaho: "When we show our respect for other living things, they respond with respect for us."

I particularly liked this one from the Apache: "All plants are our brothers and sisters. They talk to us and if we listen, we can hear them."

I knew I was hiding behind the quotes, but I preferred to think I was using them as a shield or a filter for responses until I could toss the shield aside, hopefully sometime in the near future.

Barbara was being so different around me! She approached me nearly every day, and bent over backward for my requests. It felt strange, but I felt pride too; it was almost like being a celebrity. She asked me to come talk to her group. I told her I wasn't sure. I didn't mind speaking to groups and had done it many times with stroke survivor groups, asking for United Way dollars from their advisors. I knew my stuff. I was hardly feeling like an expert on any aspect of this topic. "Flying by the seat of my pants" was more the situation.

"I could come speak *with* the group. Not sure I can talk *to* them. But why me?"

"It's a different aspect than we have emphasized, and you don't realize what a stir you are making. To think 'I knew you when.'" She winked. *Winked? The queen of passive-aggressive now winks at me.*

On my way home from work, I stopped to see Portia at the garden shop. I decided to tell her about my mole dreams. I mean, they were just moles, right? A customer was leaving as I came in, and she was helping another. I wandered around the greenhouse, finding that I was looking at the soil with a completely different lens than ever before. I imagined I was feeling the microbes burrowing and building highways under the soil. I recently read that an earthworm can grab a leaf on the surface and carry it a foot down into the dirt. *What the heck does it grab with?*

"Hi Mary! Are they talking to ya today?" Portia said.

"Ha! No, I am getting the silent treatment, I guess. Remember that first day I was in here when you commented on the mole on my arm? You said it looked like a seed pod."

"I remember, and it does."

"I have had a couple dreams about it. A while back, I had a dream it was a callus, and when I peeled it off, there was a tiny seedling of a tree growing with one small leaf at the top. I was fascinated, not scared."

"I want to have your kind of esoteric experiences! I am a botanist and I never have dreams like that!"

I continued, "The other night, I wasn't sleeping, maybe sort of meditating, and I was looking under the scab again and there was a second leaf where there'd been one."

"Ever hear of waking dreams?"

"Only by name, why?"

"Sounds like you may have had one. It's during that in-between state. You weren't asleep but not up and walking around either. You were meditating and maybe you were gifted this."

"I just can't figure out that if this is an everyday mole, why my brain is dreaming up that a tree is growing here ..." I pointed to my arm. "I often can equate dreams as metaphors for my life. I know trees are communicating with me. These just feel more real than metaphoric."

"Maybe you are tuning into Mother Earth or are on her radar. You are getting 'It's okay' messages from many sides. But I can tell ... you want to peel it back right now, don't you?" I nodded. "You had it looked at right?" I explained the somewhat sudden appearance of both moles, two doctors, the scraping, and the no cancer or even pre-cancer findings. "You said the woods had been 'watching' you, observing you for some time before you were actually approached." I nodded again. "Maybe they were preparing you. Maybe it was their portal to you, or maybe just a gift to you. It's a pretty remarkable mole. People get tattoos of their passion all the time. You were given a mark, a mark of their source, their seed. I think it's pretty fucking awesome."

"Hmmmph," was all I could muster as I processed. *Maybe I should just think of it as my mark of the woods, a tattoo. I mean, there couldn't really be a tree in my arm.* "Portia, I am so glad I stopped in. I am feeling a sense of relief at the symbology concept." I hugged and thanked her for coming into my world that short time ago.

I turned to go, when she said, "Maybe I can run something past you."

"Sure, I have the time."

"I have been noticing something between you and Jason." I just gave her a look of "mayybee." She continued, "So I am wondering if you are sensing anything yourself, uhm with ..." I jumped in, "You and Bella, hell yes."

"Would you call it mutual or just noticing me hanging it out there?"

"Oh, definitely both of you." She smiled a hopeful smile.

As I drove home, I found myself thinking about movies where the characters are thrust into a dangerous scenario, and the big battle is the next day. They have tender but urgent sex because they are clinging to safety and know it may be their last time. *Hmmmm, preparing for the big battle.*

Chapter 40

A REPORTER AT *THE SENTINEL* LEFT A MESSAGE ON my phone. He asked to interview me for an article, saying he covers environmental topics. *Who calls these days? Email me, text me. I have to call him back now.* Luckily, I procrastinated a couple days, so he sent me an email. An environmental reporter with investigative roots.

I was nervous to accept. Everyone knows they can take what parts they want and publish something slanted. Being someone slow to think of responses, God only knows what I'd say. After another day of scaring myself, I decided to respond by putting the ball in his court. I accepted with the condition that I would get the questions ahead of time by at least one day. After all, job applicants see their questions just prior to the interview. If he asked something off the list, I could decline to comment.

We emailed a couple more times and finally settled on a day the following week. I got the questions several days ahead, so I asked for a meeting of the ModQuad to help me craft answers to the questions. We even practiced answering some of them. I went to the meeting place feeling confident. I dressed as I might for work, so I presented a stronger flair than I felt. The initial several questions were on-script, and my answers were flowing like water. I was impressed with myself. It was probably his art of the craft, but I felt very comfortable with Tristin, the reporter. In hindsight, I was too comfortable. The questions and responses were going like clockwork when he started to go off-script. Next thing I knew, he was asking me how I came upon the interest in such a topic. He didn't just ask it, he seemed enthralled with the topic and put together some of the information from the previous answers and phrased it almost as if it was one of the sanctioned questions. He asked where I'd first heard of the idea that the soil was suffering. I blurted it out: "A tree communicated with me." Tristin's head jerked ever so slightly left, while his eyes widened fleetingly before regaining his composure. At that moment, I was sure his brain was calculating what his response should be if he wanted the interview to continue. What Tristin said next may have been, probably was, calculated, and it was the perfect way to snag me. His response sounded as if he believed me. "I have always thought nature is alive if we are aware enough to see it." Then I found myself elaborating more. I discovered his thinking that nature was alive wasn't the same as his believing me.

"Trees Tell Woman to Help Save the Earth's Soil" was the headline.

"Bastard!" flew out of my mouth when I saw the article online. The Squad had been watching for the article too. All my other responses were also in there, but there was no mistaking the sensationalism of that headline and my elaboration. He conveniently omitted his own statement of implied belief. He didn't make fun of me for the view. He just left that wide open for others to do. And they did.

On Twitter the next morning:

Agricorp: "Mary Keeley, the TikTok sensation, can talk to trees, she claims they talk to her too (crazy emoji). Later in the day ... "Mary Keeley, the TikTok sensation, names her trees (rolling eyes emoji).

I make so many steps forward in using my voice and feeling empowered, but I recoil so quickly. Will there be a day when I just flip the bird and say, "Yeah, so what!?" My steps had started out tiny, and I had graduated to giant steps without saying, "Mother May I?" *What does it matter?* If a sign of progress is the recovery time, then I had made solid gains. In my recoiling, I retreated to the long, hot shower. I ruminated, and in my head, I replayed the interview and re-read the headline and the Twitter comments. I was beating myself up for trusting, or maybe for not assessing the situation better, and getting sucked in. As the hot water warmed the back of my neck, I was struck with an image of Psyche and Aphrodite in my head. Psyche collapsed in tears, giving up, presuming death at the daunting task before her. With each task, she received the help she needed and moved closer to her Eros. I yanked the shower water off, dried off, dressed, and stalked off to Bella's apartment.

"Good morning, Twitter star," Bella said with a laughing smile.

"Glad you are finding it so humorous. I am pissed. I don't want to just slink away." Matt was home. Overhearing my words, he said, "Bella says you are now a sensation on two social sites!" Joining in, Bella said, "Yeah, now you just need to take it to Instagram. Facebook would hit the older folks more. You would have the corner on social networks."

Just as quickly as I was knocked down, I found myself rebounding. Someday, maybe, I wouldn't need that external infusion of strength. Nothing wrong with being helped, but maybe I wouldn't require it in order to rebound.

A text from Portia came to the Squad: "Have you seen the responses on Twitter? Take a look."

I hadn't had the nerve to go back. There were one hundred hearts and twenty-five comments. A couple referred to me as loony, but the others were acclaiming the wonderfulness of the ability, and one acknowledged the naming of trees as something commonly done by people who revere the life existing in trees. "I wonder if I should respond to the posts?" I queried as I heard a knock at the door. Matt opened it to find Jason standing there with scones and croissants. Okay, my heart leapt a teeny bit. "You weren't at your apartment, so I thought I'd check here. I am glad we all can join in the celebration of the new claim to fame." He looked at me, saying, "Hope you weren't panicking over the Twitter call-out. In my business of challenging the established powers, it's a sign of getting to them." For me, this was a moment like watching clouds that shift shapes. What had slingshot me back to the all-familiar emotions of dread and fear had made its own shift to pride. I was picking up the baton being handed to me.

"That's what I told her, now let's hit Instagram and Facebook!" Bella said. And we did. We got Portia to join us. We brainstormed what words to use to respond. The room's energy was kinetic. We started a fan page. We made the Apache quote front and center: "All plants are our brothers and sisters. They talk to us and if we listen, we can hear them."

We copied the tweets. It presented the supposition that many people have the ability to hear nature. We responded to the original tweet with the same quote.

Chapter 41

A S I ENTERED THE WOODS, I FELT A presence I hadn't felt before. My usual wash of calm was replaced with a gut alert. I passed Matt. Had his expression changed? The lips looked tighter. His eyes were narrower, not big and round as if seeing the world with wonder. I smiled and waved, thinking trees change, too, as creatures peck here and there or nature's own forces alter them. What I didn't know was that he was sending a signal throughout the forest. I don't usually ignore that gut alarm; it had served me well during times of vetting creepy guys or creepy situations I was entering. However, I normally felt so embraced by the woods that it didn't occur to me.

As I stepped past the Warrior, I heard a twig clip somewhere behind me. I turned but saw no creature. My gut alarm sounded louder, and I hastened along the trail. Coming from behind me, I heard, "Shit! Damn tree." There was a creature, not one I knew. Definitely male. I know these woods best, and I moved off-trail, but stealthiness wasn't my best trait. I had hoped to see whoever passed by. He must have stopped as I did. I moved through the brush. *I should move out, but he is more likely to see me.* I could hear movement following mine. I tried to think quickly and decided to work my way back to Populus Tremulous and Emmiline. I picked up a thick stick from the floor of the woods. *Better than nothing.* Being deeper in the woods but right across from Populus, with a probably unwarranted sense of safety, I moved closer to the path.

I heard a soft, sick-sounding quiet singing, "Witchy-witchy, where are you?" A man emerged within ten feet of me, wearing camo pants and brandishing a knife. His hair hadn't been combed in weeks, his teeth were dirty. I must have gotten complacent, not tending to my gut detector. This guy's energy would have normally alerted me blocks away.

"I am right here, fucker!" I equally brandished my stick as I stepped onto the path. It might be able to keep him away.

"So, you talk to trees and they talk to you. Only a witch could do such a thing."

"What century are you from? You do know what year it is, right?" I wielded my stick to keep him from seeing how much I was trembling. Thank God my voice was holding steady.

"You probably made that log surge and come down on my shin." I noticed his pant leg was torn.

"So that's why you are limping. I do have some friends in this forest. And why do you think I am a witch?"

"Witches could use nature's forces to harm people."

"I think you have it backward. Humans have used human forces to harm nature for at least a couple centuries now."

As he took steps toward me, I matched them in the other direction. "You are all over the internet. Sooner or later, others will join you. It needs to stop here."

"So, you are not disputing that nature can communicate with us. You just don't like it."

"It's wrong. God tells us what we need, gives us what we need. Nature doesn't."

Two things happened simultaneously. The ground heaved and roots rose up, knocking this jerk backward and to the ground. And Bella appeared from what seemed to be thin air and was standing over him, pointing a high-powered rifle, with one foot on his wrist that was holding the knife. She bent toward him, feeling for other weapons. She didn't find any. Seething, she spoke, "Thomas, this is over right now. You need to crawl back under your rock, never to be seen again around my apartment, these woods, or this person." He dropped the knife so Bella would release her foot. The wind picked up, and he was surrounded by fireflies that literally flipped him to his knees. His eyes showed terror along with disbelief. "You are just like her, Bella. You always have been."

"Then I would surely get the hell out of here before we conjure up better things for you!" He stumbled forward, using his hands as he wobbled to his feet. He ran out of the woods. Bella picked up the knife and stuck it, along with her gun, in the shoulder harness.

Staring at Bella in disbelief, I said, "Where did you come from, how did you know? Who the hell is he?"

"He is my ex."

"That's your husband? I'd always pictured someone with a bit more stature."

"Ex, not husband. I said he was a survivalist sort. Never said he was particularly good at the skill of it. Never said he was hot. Pretty much always a chicken shit trying to act tough. Bullying was what he did best; it took me too long to see it."

"Same question, where did you come from and how did you know?"

"I got a message from the forest. My plants were abuzz. Apparently, I have reclaimed my worthiness. I knew you were in trouble, I just didn't know what kind. I eventually saw Thomas lurking behind you and followed him; he had no idea. I was much better at his game than he was and definitely more than he ever thought. He felt stealthiness was a male quality and a female could never master the woods. The same patriarchal mistake has been made by men for eons."

Shifting my eyes around, I replied, "I had projected I might get pushback from big agribusiness. Hadn't anticipated the patriarchy would rise up."

"Do you think they are different forces? It's so entrenched, one has to read and dig deep to find where they separate."

"Welcome back, Bella. This is an unanticipated surprise." Our heads swung to look at Emmiline, then to each other. "Bella, you heard that?" She nodded a beaming smile. I challenged, "What did you hear, tell me." She repeated the words. I slipped to the ground, laid back, and giggled. "Okay, what's behind that?" Bella questioned.

Laughing, I said, "It is officially confirmed: I am not crazy. Even though I was embracing this gift, there was still a corner in my brain telling me I had a tumor or was going insane. Now at least I am not alone in my head."

We sat with Emmiline for some time. "There is a sense of optimism throughout the underground avenues, as if someone is listening and things are changing. Knowing there's a new effort is making us stronger. We are hearing messages from a number of fronts, including children, farmers, and budding activists."

As we walked out of the woods, we both heard the chattering among the trees that neither of us had heard before. We reached Warrior and sure enough, he was angled differently across the path. Something had shifted. I stopped and touched his decaying bark. "I don't know if being dead is the same in tree life as in human life, but I thank you, however you managed to intervene."

We reached Matt and his expression was as it had always been. He no longer looked worried. I knew now that he'd been the one to send the alarm. I stood close and hugged him, once again thanking him for standing sentry. My body warmed in the way that human arms around me would evoke.

As we emerged from the woods, I said, "Do you think it's true that we are making a difference? Is something really starting?"

Bella responded, "I remember when people started saying no to GMOs, it seemed that companies scrambled to change their labeling. It didn't matter if their product had corn or not. It didn't matter whether they ever used GMOs or not, their packaging now had 'Non-GMO' written in big letters. Now most people at least know what GMOs are, even if they aren't concerned. When people started demanding more organic products, grocery store chains began issuing their own brand of organic products. Surely it happens over a period of time, but if a large enough effort is sustained for long enough, the people can influence business practices."

She continued, "Sorry about Thomas. I never saw the need to tell you all he was. I thought he was long gone from here."

"I am trying not to let my brain overreact to this. Already, I find myself thinking if he was lurking, watching, what if someone with more harmful intent is too? You can't always be there; I can't always be in my forest."

"You know the adage, prepare for the worst, hope for the best."

"Obviously, I am not very prepared. I never liked emotional conflict or confrontations. I am a 'let's talk it out' kind of person. This is rising to a different level."

Chapter 42

I REACHED FOR MY PHONE AND CALLED KELLY. I remember chuckling when Kelly came into the woods with me, toting her gun. "Hey Kelly, how are you?"

"How are YOU, is the question. I have been meaning to call you. You are making a splash on all sorts of social media platforms."

"That splash is exactly the reason I am calling. I am wondering how you got your concealed carry license. I want to believe I am over-reacting but also don't want to be naive."

"Did something happen? I am sensing a tinge of panic in your voice."

"As only you would notice, you empath." After a deep breath, I reiterated the story about the lean-to and how it turned out that the ex-husband of the woman who built it is rankled by the events of recent. "He called me a witch, came at me with a knife."

"Honey, you are entering new territory! Preparedness should be your next step. It was a class. Surprisingly easy and quick to get. I suppose you have to start with getting a gun."

"Even that sounds uncomfortable. So many people seem to think they need all levels of armed protection. It is so against my belief system. Maybe I should try some other form of self-defense. I may be more the bow and arrow sort of defender."

"Have you ever shot a gun?"

"A couple times in my 'previous life.'"

"Let's do this ... Let's go to the shooting range and you can see what it's like to handle my size of gun. You may be able to better decide."

I was shooting Kelly's Browning Hi-Power 9 mm handgun. I had forgotten the fun factor in doing this. Of course, one has to take it seriously, but the range reminded me a bit of Top Golf or a bowling alley. It was definitely a false sense of power that came from stepping into a different world and shooting a gun. It ran along the same line of learning any skill that provides some independence as a woman. I likened it to being able to change your own tire or fix a leak. Something I traditionally look to a man to do.

I shifted my view of Thomas to being an anomaly. Most opposition would probably come in the form of ridicule and intimidation. Big agribusiness isn't going to send some thug after me. They will send their lawyers if they sense any threat at all to their bottom line.

Even with my thoughts going in that direction, Kelly and I scheduled a second trip to the shooting range for next week. Then I would decide if I really wanted to have a gun in my apartment, let alone on my person.

The next day at work, Barbara reminded me her group wanted to set a date for me to come speak. Question-and-answer-like, she assured me. I got an email from Regen Farms, an organization of Regenerative Farmers that Jason had contacted, inviting me to sit in on their next meeting. Lance, who wrote the letter, indicated all members feel that caring for the quality of the earth's soil is a driving force of their practices. The byproduct was improved crops. He also wanted me to know there were some members who felt the earth communicated with them also.

That last piece made my day. *If I am not alone in this and others have had the gift but not stepped forward, I need to suck it up and speak my truth. Let the chips fall where they may.*

Chapter 43

THE MODQUAD GOT TOGETHER OVER DRINKS AFTER WORK on Friday. I told them about the conversation with Bella regarding businesses changing when the masses start buying a specific type of product. I added that even McDonald's and Burger King changed when people didn't want so much sugar and when Beyond Burgers went big. More recently, grass-fed beef and pasture-raised chicken are available in nearly every store. What if we could get people to care what kind of soil their crops were grown in? Portia joined in, illuminating that one of the main reasons people don't buy organic or grass-fed products is due to the cost. "Not everyone CAN pay extra for the quality element. Just getting food on the table is enough of a struggle. What if the products grown from regenerative farming practices could be sold at the SAME price as products supported by agribusinesses?" Bella leaned over and kissed her on the cheek. "GREAT idea!" *Don't change my expression, don't change my expression.*

"I love, LOVE that idea!" I said. "Hey Bella, want to give the update on the forest's latest message?" Bella recounted, starting out nonchalantly with, "I ran into my ex in the forest the other day ... ground rising up ..." We ended the recounting with a toast to witches, real and perceived. Jason was staring at me with a look between wild-eyed and disbelief. I jumped in with the addition that I'd gone with my friend, Kelly, to the shooting range and had another time scheduled next week and that I might get a concealed weapons permit. Bella and Portia both got up to go pee and Jason immediately said, "Can't believe what almost happened to you, AND that you didn't tell me about it."

Questioningly, I asked, "Are you worried for my safety, upset you didn't save me, or that I didn't tell you?"

"Not sure, maybe some boy-saves-girl stuff hidden in there."

"Please, that role is neither necessary nor welcomed. I will gladly take an accomplice. I guess you could meet me at the shooting range?" *Why do I feel the need to say that?*

"Even though it's not widely known in my IWO circle, I do hunt. I know how to shoot. If your friend can't make it, I am game to go with you. I do own a handgun."

Bella and Portia sat down looking quite satisfied and overhearing the conversation. "Jason, you hunt? What do you hunt?"

"Birds ... duck, turkey. Fish." He chuckled. It led to a whole different string of views of hunting versus fishing, and why one seems to carry more criticism than the other.

Chapter 44

I FELT NERVOUS SITTING IN ON THE ZOOM MEETING with the Regenerative Farmers. I had no idea what to expect. There was a range of ages from young to quite elderly. More and more, I realized age plays no part in reverence for the earth. It spanned from the youngest to the oldest. Of the fifteen people on the call, there was one other woman. I was honored by their openness to my efforts. After a report out about business practices and where regenerative farming was getting press, the conversation switched to how their crops were faring this time of year. Then one of them asked me how I was sensing the communication with the trees. Noting my silence and scanning the faces on the screen, Lance assured me none of them thought I was insane and that a couple of them had experienced similar events, although not ongoing. These experiences were enough to provide inspiration for their farming direction. I said the best way I could explain it was a sort of mental telepathy, in which we heard each other without speaking. One of the older gentlemen asked a younger one, named Trent, to tell me about his dream. I was stunned by what I heard. He seemed a bit timid but started with holding his left shoulder up to the camera to show a mole.

He said, "This mole just kind of showed up. I don't know if I hadn't had that angle in the mirror or what, but one day, I was rubbing on sunscreen and felt this mole. I have had it checked out by two doctors, but no one thinks it is anything to be alarmed by. So, I just let it be. Then one night I had a dream. It was one of those that is so real that you are surprised when you wake up and recognize you were dreaming. I was sitting looking at the mole, but in the dream, it had become callused. I couldn't resist peeling it off, and when I did, there was a mushroom inside, emerging from the soil. I know that sounds crazy, but it seemed so real. After that, I had a couple experiences in which I was digging in the dirt and I was greeted by a voice asking me to take better care of the soil."

I held my forearm up to the camera. "I know exactly what you are talking about. Mine isn't setting alarms off in the medical community either. I, too, had a dream, but inside my mole was a tree seedling with a small leaf growing from the top. To add to all that, I have met a botanist, and when she first saw the mole, she likened it to a seedpod. Do you mind if I take a screenshot of your mole and show it to her?"

"No, please do. I'd be curious for sure. I will type my email in the chat box so you have it. Let me know what she says!" he said with a sweet expression telling me he felt understood.

Chapter 45

KELLY AND I WENT BACK TO THE SHOOTING range. I think Jason was a bit disappointed to not be needed. I was liking the girl power we were generating. I had always taken instruction better from female peers than male, especially males I have had sex with. Kelly was a very good shot. She had always been one of those hidden athletes. Much more capable than expected when looking at her. I definitely improved over the first time. Maybe it would be fun to come with Jason in the near future. I didn't care about being sniper quality, but I wanted to know enough to make the next lunatic recognize this girl knew her way around a gun.

The following week, I went to Barbara's group. It wasn't quite as comfortable since they seemed to view me a bit more as a celebrity. I didn't want any pedestals, even though I should be happy that I was inspiring something in them. We talked about farming practices, both good and bad. They explained their focus is primarily on our bodies' depleted systems, since our foods don't carry the nutrients that they did decades ago. They brought up that the average person can't afford to spend money on more conscientiously raised food. We talked about what we all can do in backyard gardens and ways I'd learned to augment even potted plants. It was interesting to watch

Barbara in a different setting. She was lighthearted and jovial. In other words, nothing like her work persona. It occurred to me that maybe, no matter how it started for her, she was no longer walking the path that fed her soul. What I dealt with ... had dealt with, at work was the outward manifestation of just that. I knew my burnout manifested in situational depression and withdrawal. Too often, we never have the time to peel the layers of someone else's burnout.

Eventually, we got around to the tree talking thing. Everybody was fascinated with that. Now that I was owning it, it really had become very fun for me. The trees were my friends. Belief in nature communicating with us was much older and more common than many might think. The woman next to me, Molly, rolled up her sleeves as she was speaking. I couldn't help but notice a large protruding mole on her arm. I was trying not to stare at it, but when the meeting was over, I immediately turned to her, "Excuse me, but I couldn't help but notice your mole." She self-consciously but quickly put down her sleeve. "I don't mean to be intrusive or call out something that is sensitive. I have a feeling you have had it checked out by possibly more than one doctor; I suspect it is fairly new. My real question is if you have ever seen inside it as a piece of a dream?"

Looking surprised, she nodded, "Right on all accounts, and yes, I have had a dream about it."

"Can I try to guess its content?"

"Yes, but I doubt you will, it's pretty bizarre."

"It was small but there was something plant-based growing inside."

"Holy crap! Yes, it was an echinacea plant. How did you know that?"

I showed her my mole, and said, "A small tree, at first with one leaf, now two."

"So, it's grown!" she exclaimed. I nodded, "I know, even more bizarre. Continuing on with bizarro, I have met yet another person who has experienced the same thing." Beaming, she responded, "So I am part of an elite forces group."

I shrugged. "There is some force at work for sure. Do you mind if I take a photo of it?" I explained the botanist friend connection and her telling me the mole resembled a seed pod more than a mole. She let me take the photo. I assured her it wouldn't end up online, adding, "I like the idea of seedpod versus mole. Sounds friendly, not ominous like a new mole can be." I put her contact info in my phone and texted her, so she had mine. Reassuring her, I emphasized, "Let's keep in touch about this. We must be meeting for a reason."

Chapter 46

I STOPPED TO SEE PORTIA THE NEXT DAY. I told her about the people I'd met and asked if she could ID the moles as resembling anything in nature. She did. One spore of a mushroom, the other a flower seed.

"What do you think this means, Portia? Beyond nature alerting us, waking us?"

"You are finding each other for a reason, but hell if I know what it is. It's too much of an anomaly not to be significant and foretelling. Hey, by the way, now that you are out there talking to groups, why don't you come with me to the local chapter of botanists. That's not being totally honest, they really want you to come and tell your story. It's making people feel excited and understood in a way beyond someone just loving to garden. Like the earth is affirming we have been on the right path all along. Will you come?"

"Sure, why not."

When I got home, I sent an email to Trent from the farmers group, attaching a photo of the mushroom spore and telling him what Portia had said. Then I sent a text to Molly with a photo of an echinacea seed. They must have been waiting; they both responded instantaneously, thanking me profusely for helping them feel part of something bigger instead of something freakish.

I had the next day off, and I packed a bag enough to spend the morning in the woods. I settled down with greeting cowboy Populus Tremulous, even though I knew he wasn't sensing me anymore. I realized I had come to love Emmiline just as much. She, like Barbara, was so much more than what I initially saw.

Emmiline started, "How are you coping with your new fame?"

"Right now, it's pretty fun. Never would have predicted me feeling this way, but once I started to own what I have experienced, things shifted." I continued talking, telling her about the two people with moles I had met and asked her if she had any idea why we are being brought together.

She went into the hundredth monkey concept. If a behavior or belief is repeated for long enough, it's morphic resonance affects the entire species. She continued on regarding their efforts to find those people who will pick up the baton. "If enough people can lead their groups in the same direction, eventually they converge. That's where you come in."

"How's that?"

"You are the one encountering the different groups. With you, they will more likely converge with one message. When you include the people you have been educating on your social media, you are amassing a great number."

"Yeah, the groups are approaching soil from different angles, but they all want the same thing … to help the earth, help people to recognize the value of soil, for people to stop disturbing it and poisoning it, to understand the life it holds, and to realize that it can improve our lives." Jason's image came into my head as it suddenly occurred to me that I had a scientist right under my nose. My lips curled up as I thought about the warming image of him physically under more than my nose. I pushed the thought out of my head for now. Business first.

Emmiline began talking about the increased number of visitors to the woods.

Surprised, I asked, "What kind of visitors?"

"I'd say curious people. A tremendous amount of head turning and tree gazing. Seemed honoring."

"Glad to hear that but not thrilled to have more company."

"I would try to consider them as allies. They have come to experience something for which they are longing. This forest was here long ago and with care will continue to be. Better to have it filled with people who revere it and tread lightly." She was making a good point. *I am basically asking to lose my solitude every time I tell my story.*

"If this movement expands, maybe there'd be more woods protected in the future." We sat in silence for some time. I began thinking about next steps. How to reach more groups. How to bring groups together. How to get agribusiness to pause and rethink their practices. That one sounded daunting.

When I got back to my apartment, I started thinking what else, beyond my story, I might want to ask of the botanist's chapter. *It's time I start directing where this will go since I now know I have their attention.*

I texted Jason: "Feel like a beer?"

"Naturally. When? Public or private? (shit-eating grin emoji)"

"Let's start public (thinking monocle emoji). Tomorrow after work?"

He texted back: "There's a bar with a great patio down the street from my condo. It's Nacho Place. Hope you like nachos, that's all they have. 6:00?"

"See you there."

We met the next night. Nacho Place had a fun vibe with ten nacho choices in small, medium, and large. Large being amazing ingredients embedded in what must have been a complete bag of tortilla chips. We sat in the warmth of the sun. It's not that I hadn't thought of the day in the forest many times, but it was apparent it was on Jason's mind as hopefully the primary purpose of this meeting. The disappointment was palpable when I said Portia and Bella were joining us in an hour.

"Jason, I have definitely thought about that day too. Can I assume you have?"

"Hmmmm. Maybe more than you have." His eyes flickered. "I did pick this place knowing it was very near my condo."

Nodding my head, I said, "That wasn't completely lost on me. I do want to talk to you as a business partner first."

"Talk fast," he chuckled. I proceeded to tell him I'd realized I was minus a scientific expert in this equation. I had read up but certainly needed a scientist to explain the urgency of our message and to respond to the pushback we were bound to start receiving. I needed someone who could speak the jargon. I asked him to pair up with me, to possibly attend Portia's group with me, but particularly to attend others that may transpire. To be a link between the beauty of the trees talking to me and the reality of why it's necessary.

He took my hand from across the table and looked seriously into my eyes. "My speaking fees are not cheap, ya know." With that, he took a napkin from the table and asked me if I had a pen in my purse. He wrote something on the napkin and slid it my way, gazing at me the entire time. Feeling pretty sure there wasn't a dollar figure on the napkin, that this was not a monetary exchange, I slowly unfolded it. I looked up at him as I did so.

"My place, my way."

Shaking my head and smirking a chuckle, I said, "And here I thought you just really cared about the environment."

Looking over his beer, he replied, "I can multitask, but I think I made my desire clear early on. Deal?"

I held out my hand, "Deal, but it doesn't go into effect until I have seen how worthwhile your performance is."

As he shook my hand, he held my gaze, "Oh it will be worth the effort and worth your while."

Thank God Portia and Bella walked in. We caught up about the week. Jason said he was heading to the men's room. After he walked away, Bella looked at me, "Holy cow, what did we walk in the middle of?" Shaking my head as if coming out of a trance, I simply spoke "Oh my" before Portia saw Jason on his way back. "God, men are fast."

"What did I miss?"

Bella jumped in, "Hardly gone long enough to miss anything. I was going to tell you all that Matt's mom's hearing was today, and they continued their denial of parent rights. It's not reviewed again for three months. I just don't think she's staying clean."

"Oh, poor guy. That must be very disappointing. How is he doing?"

"Interestingly, I think he has mixed feelings. His social worker can't say much, but I think there was some fairly serious neglect going on for a while. I think his mom wants to be good, wants him in her life, and loves him in the best way an addict can. He has told me he feels happy at this current school and that feeling happy hasn't been much a part of his life for some time. He's actually developed friendships and his teacher thinks he's quite bright. He also has said he is sleeping better than he could for a long time. I must say I will be sad to have him go when he does. He is very kind and appreciative. Nice to have a child around, although some days he sounds more like a little adult. I imagine he has seen many things that have required him to grow up beyond the typical eleven-year-old."

I chimed in with, "As you are talking, it occurs to me it could be good to have Matt attend some presentations. He is wise, and it's his generation we are ultimately going to need to understand and to see this through. Are there rules about what events you can attend with him?"

Chapter 47

WHEN PORTIA INTRODUCED ME TO THE GROUP OF botanists, I saw such anticipation on their faces. It was the oddest feeling to recognize that it was *my* words they were anticipating. I started with my story of visiting some nearby woods and always seeing faces in trees. I mentioned the fireflies, and the day of the winds, and the first time Populus Tremulous communicated to me. I explained I had chosen the word communication because it's not like they talk with mouths, harkening back to the apple trees in *The Wizard of Oz* or the Ents in *Lord of the Rings*. I described it as an unspoken conversation.

I asked if others in the group had ever experienced nature communicating with them. There were forty in the group, and at least half of the hands went up. I asked if anyone wanted to tell their own story. Many hands went up. We spent fifteen minutes with people sharing an array of messages. They spanned from flowers and plants letting them know when they needed water, to asking to be moved to another place in the house or garden, to informing them their soil needed augmenting. I thanked them for sharing so openly and asked if they'd shared this with many people. Few had. The potential ridicule had kept them quiet. They felt liberated and part of a growing group that had more members than they ever dreamed.

I moved on to my more recent discovery of other groups who also have members who at least sense what nature needs. Talking almost out loud to myself, I said that in order to make a lasting difference with this, we need to find ways to impact both production and sales of food. Impacting agribusinesses would best be done by slowing the purchasing of items produced with soil-damaging products and practices. With that, I introduced Jason. I mentioned he worked for the IWO, had a background in bioengineering, and could explain the long-term impact of unsustainable farming.

He began explaining that biology is the study of life. His recent focus had been on the study of life in the soil. He referred to a piece of information from Kristin Ohlson's *The Soil Will Save Us*, indicating that often when soil samples are taken, they are mistakenly taken in problem spots, indicating that it is equally important to analyze the soil that is thriving. We must find out what makes it thrive. He explained in a simple language how thriving soil sequesters soil and retains water. Most of these botanists had begun to hear about using cover crops to hold the nutrients over the winter and allow the soil to continue developing. It was a new-ish discovery for me. I was definitely planning to bring him to all my meetings, which brought our deal to mind.

As the meeting finished up, a young woman came up to me and quietly asked if she could share another thing with me. We stepped away from the crowd, and she held up her forearm. There was a small, dark, slender mark.

I didn't bat an eye seeing a mole, asking, "What did it look like in your dream?"

Surprised but matter-of-fact, she said, "A budding cosmos. Do you know what those are? They're a delicate-looking flower with pastel petals, but they are hearty beyond their appearance. But how did you know?"

"Believe me, you are not alone. I am starting to wonder how many there are of us. Counting you and me, I know of four now." I had to add, "Presuming it's fairly new, you have had it looked at right? Just in case?" She had received the same non-concerned medical responses. "Do you know if the mole resembles the seed of that flower?" She said it did. "Do you mind showing it to Portia? She's seen the others only in photos."

I caught Portia's eye and motioned her over. Amelia held her arm out, and Portia knew what to look at. "A cosmos seed, sweet. Welcome to an elite subset."

As the meeting broke up, the present squad members stood in the parking lot. I called Bella and put her on speaker. I said, "I am feeling there are so many threads to this adventure. We have us ... the squad, a boy, the farmers, the horticulturists, a scientist, and the mole people. What does it all mean? What do we focus on? How are we to bring them together and do something with it all?"

I had decided that Bella was the sage of our group. The sense maker. "You may have answered your own question. What is that thing, that denominator, that will make agribusiness shift their efforts away from unnatural practices? The bottom line is it's not that businesses start out to make products that will destroy something or make people sick. They discover something that answers a need like pesticide-resistant seeds and plants, and then they are so entrenched in profits, someone in charge digs in deeper, touting the benefit and diminishing the risk. Or the risks are determined to be less than their benefit."

I needed to be up the next day for work, so I had to head home. We agreed to create a forward momentum plan next time we met. As I laid in bed wide awake, I got to thinking about each of the people with moles. If my being selected by Cowboy related to my ability to communicate and subsequently to bring people together, maybe each of them had a voice that could lead their individual group. We were the message carriers.

Chapter 48

THE NEXT TIME THE SQUAD MET, WE LAID out our plan. We made a list of regenerative farmers. We would each post who they were, who they distributed to, and the benefit of the farming method to the soil. I would schedule a meeting with the Message Carriers, asking them to further the conversation with their respective groups.

I met the next week with the Message Carriers via Zoom. We initially introduced ourselves, and of course, we had to look at each other's moles, what I later started referring to as "marks of the messengers." In detailing each of our dreams, we discovered they were remarkably similar. I shared my story of being selected for this journey due to my ability to communicate. I was extrapolating that they each had a similar ability. They responded much as I had, somewhat of a "Who me?" astonishment. I talked about the concept of being "big in a room." I was always the quiet observer of a crowd, most comfortable in a small gathering, finding my voice primarily with those who knew me best. This resonated with each of them, and they began questioning, "What's being asked of me?"

Each had a statement similar to Trent's: "What really is the message we are giving? I get scared in front of a group." I advised what I'd learned. We could push our comfort levels somewhat, but we would do best if we found the path that felt like a natural progression. I reminded them that they already were attending meetings of like-minded people, and could start with their groups. We were all working, so we could consider sharing with colleagues at our jobs. The idea was to make agribusiness notice that people are choosing more natural foods, people want the earth to be healthy, and they want the soil to thrive. We searched the internet and found articles about the use of regenerative farming and soil practices being used in everything from cattle raising to gardens in The Battery in NY City. We found that regenerative practices were being used internationally.

We ended up in agreement that everyone would find one comfortable manner to communicate something about the soil, whether it be the challenge of the soil, the value of the soil, or best practices for enriching the soil.

The response was more than we had dreamed. Two knew people in other countries, so those friends shared the information with others who knew people in yet other countries. It was spreading like a web, and the six degrees of separation were incredible. The Squad and the Messengers spent more time together as a group, analyzing the responses and determining the next steps. Regenerative farmers were seeing a surge in their sales. They had new people attending their chapter meetings. Jason was speaking to more groups and rocking every one. IWO profiled him in their national newsletter. He spoke more and more about the value of leaving the soil as-is by respecting the synergy between plants and organisms, versus upsetting the balance that the microbes created naturally.

It was getting hard for me to find time to work. Before patients started to notice my distraction, I took a three-month leave of absence. I was loving my new purpose in communication. My level of enthusiasm reminded me of my first years as an SLP, when it didn't matter how long I worked or how busy I was. Amelia was most impressive. She was only in her twenties and so articulate, rising beyond expectations. Young passion, ahhhh, I do remember it. She was feeling pride in finding her voice. We had all found our voices. Trent had organized a website clearinghouse listing the regenerative farmers registered by state. He remained behind the scenes but was a driving force in the ease of access for people. The remarkable thing he accomplished was a co-op of products which were sent to food banks so all economic levels could experience the nutrition of organic food. It was historically priced out of reach for lower income people, and certainly those on food stamps. He also managed to inspire a few local chain markets to provide these products to people on food stamps at the price of regular foods. The impact went both up the supply chain and down. Community gardens were rethinking their soil and planning cover crops for the fall. More parks and university grounds were looking to places like Harvard, where eighty-five acres were managed organically. It was a section where the ground had been compacted due to foot traffic, and trees were dying. Now roots were finding plenty of room to expand for water and oxygen.

One day, I received a phone call from a man who claimed to work for Curacorp in their Soil Division. I would have thought I was being pranked, but he did speak with a French accent, and caller ID also confirmed it was from France. He stated that he was calling on behalf of his boss, who was traveling to America on business and requested to meet with me. When I asked how he had heard of me and what the meeting was about, he explained that our message had made its way to France and subsequently caught the eye of their marketing and legal departments. Ms. Blanc would be in New York City, and asked if I would be willing to meet with her if they flew me there. I indicated I needed to be clearer on the agenda before I agreed, and that I wouldn't be comfortable doing this alone. I would want my team there also. I said "four" when asked how many that would be. I added, "Would lawyers be there?" He said no, it was a meeting of interest, not a meeting of confrontation.

I left it with, "Send me something in writing, find out if my colleagues can attend too, and I will get back to you."

I received an email the following day from Ms. Blanc.

Dear Ms. Keeley,

I hope this letter finds you well. My assistant informed me you wanted clarification on my invitation for a meeting. You have made quite the splash in France. Our country's farming practices, and overall belief in maintaining the soil's integrity, is gaining attention. I head up the soil restoration division and am hoping we can be allies versus each other's antagonists. I recognize big agribusiness is probably not on your traditional list of favorites, nor on many constituents. Curacorp is doing some innovative work and positive awareness would be helpful.

My intent will be purely to share what work we are doing and hopefully make it clear we are not a nemesis. As far as arrangements, I will fly you and your team to NYC and provide accommodations at the Hilton hotel. We will dine at Graziers. My schedule is tight, and I recommend Wednesday the 15th of this month.

I look forward to hearing from you. If this is feasible, I will have my assistant contact you for details.

Sincerely,

Emma Blanc

I ran upstairs to show the email to Bella. She was excited but indicated she probably couldn't go and leave Matt behind or in another's care. I was frustrated with myself since he was clearly such a force in the beginning of this. "Can he take a trip with you? If so, I will say, 'Sorry, it's five not four.' She seemed very motivated to meet us. Big business wants some good press." Bella was able to get a court order approving her to take Matt with her to New York.

The five of us were flown to the city and provided a shuttle to the hotel. I'd checked out the restaurant, and we decided business attire was warranted. Matt was excited to travel, as he'd never been out of his county, let alone out of state.

Even though he adored Matt, Jason was visibly disappointed when he discovered he was bunking with Matt instead of me, freeing up Portia and Bella to share a room. "Do I need to remind you of my fee?" he whispered in my ear, lingering there for an added breath.

"You do not. This isn't 'your place' and we need to focus tonight before the 'big game.'"

"You can handle this in your sleep by now, but I will yield since the earth is at stake."

We were taxied to the restaurant, which happened to be next to the Ritz where Ms. Blanc was staying. Getting out of the taxi, Bella remarked, "Business must be very good." After introductions, Ms. Blanc asked us to call her Emma. *Good start.* Emma proceeded to order a bottle of chardonnay and chocolate milk for Matt. She didn't ask us if we liked white, but truly none of us was that picky. Her confidence and a kind formality exuded from every pore. She didn't appear more than fifty. I momentarily envied how she must not have been raised in an atmosphere of self-doubt and limiting beliefs. I let the thought pass since we all find our way in our own time.

I was glad Jason was there to vet her information. He asked about their purchase of Biocide Enterprises and her eyes flickered briefly but her words didn't skip a beat. You could tell it wasn't her favorite corporate decision either. We all judged her as sincere. Surprisingly, she asked that if we believed and liked her information, that Cura-corp be part of one of the TikTok videos, even suggesting a song for the background. She had a young niece who would get a kick out of it. She mentioned something about Bella being Matt's mom, and he was quick to inform her that Bella was his foster mom. Emma apologized, saying they looked very connected. She added, "I spent a couple years in foster care, and I hope things will work out for the best, as they did for me." He nodded and said, "I am very happy these days."

It was apparent Emma had done some homework prior to meeting us, since she knew I was a speech pathologist, Portia an owner of a garden store, and Jason worked for IWO. Our heads all turned to Bella when she mentioned Bella's history as a wing walker on a biplane stunt team. *How did THAT never come up?!* She looked sheepishly proud and indicated it was a lifetime ago.

We flew back home the next morning. I was seated next to Jason, and he slipped me another napkin with "My place on ___?" written on it. I took out a pen and wrote, "Saturday, at 7?" His smile showed he was clinging to his composure and leaned in for a quick kiss. Matt, sitting across the aisle, said, "I get in trouble for passing notes." Even though we knew full well we were adults, we both felt sheepish.

"Anything I should know about the 'my way' part of the first negotiation?"

"Mary, I respect you and have the best of intentions for us both. Let me have some mystery. Without sounding too boorish, I would love it if you wore a skirt. Make it a short one."

I went into the woods the next day, wanting to tell Emmiline about going to New York, but somehow, I wondered if she already knew it.

As soon as I walked up, she said, "See, you are much more than you knew. The network is feeling a resurgence of life. We are breathing again."

With my heart wide open, I said, "I must thank you too. Yes, I have found a purpose I haven't experienced in forever. Even more so, I have found a tribe I felt I was meant to meet. You and Populus's belief in me was something I'd never felt so rawly. I remain in awe of how I was picked, but I do feel I am doing a pretty damn good job."

As I walked out of my woods, I caught myself looking up and around, noticing versus grounding. I let all the changes of these past months roll around inside, acknowledging the edges that had smoothed, the cells that had awakened, and the appreciation of life. I would continue this path for the earth but would also explore that speech pathology private practice to keep serving people in their ability to communicate.

●●●

As I got dressed, I felt a little twinge of anxiety, which I identified as both titillating and worrisome. *What does "my way" mean exactly?* Adjusting my short skirt, I rang Jason's doorbell. As he opened the door, the smell of baking lasagna wafted out. Soft music reached my ears, and I had a fleeting thought he had seen me coming, since John Legend's new CD had just started on *Ooh Laa*. I scanned his apartment, relieved to see no overt signs of any adult toys, and pleased to see adult-like furniture instead of a man cave. Wine was breathing on the table next to a small vase of flowers. He gestured me in with a slow sweep of his arm. As I passed by him, he kissed me lightly on the back of the neck while shutting the door.

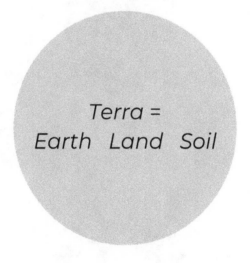

Terra =
Earth   Land   Soil

About the Author

Nancy Houser-Bluhm has lived in the foothills west of Denver, Colorado, for over twenty years with her husband and miscellaneous pets. She hails from Michigan but always had a longing for the mountains after growing up watching *Bonanza*. Their current piece of heaven is called the Bluhmerosa. For some years, she and her husband, Jon, traversed the country, living in Michigan, Oregon, and Colorado. Once a rock climber, she now spends time biking, skiing, camping, enjoying nature, and yoga; oh, yes, and writing.

Nancy received her first monetary writing award of $3.00 for a poem submitted by her middle school. About the same time, she won a statewide essay contest which took her to a presidential inauguration. She realizes she has outed herself and can never again use attending a presidential inauguration in the party game One Truth, Two Lies.

Authentic communication with herself and others has been an ultimate life quest, sometimes to the chagrin of others. What began with journaling led to publishing her own journal, Minderings ©, developed with her husband's art. She's been published numerous times in a local newspaper. After working for forty years as a speech-language pathologist, both in schools and health care, she retired from being a full-time worker bee. It was then that she began a blog and ventured into the arena of writing *Whispers for Terra*, her first novel.

Author photo © Cheryl Miller

Acknowledgments

I have been humbled and honored by the interest, support, and generosity of so many people throughout this exciting and daunting undertaking. Thanks to the people who asked me how the writing was going during those days when I was still uncomfortable to bring up "I'm writing a book" in conversation. Thanks to the people who were open to brainstorming the storyline over and over. Then there were those who were responsive to ponderings, no matter how many times I changed the title of the story, my logo, or my cover.

I should first thank Tami Jurgens-Styles for actually assuming I would follow through on my retirement message that I wanted to replace report writing as a speech pathologist with creative writing. It was her numerous out-of-the-blue texts that were the initial impetus for walking the book-writing journey.

Sage Adderley-Knox serendipitously popped into my email with her Idea to Outline seminar that got the journey going, and she encouragingly stuck with me through every single "stuck" moment over the next year as my writing process mentor.

My beta readers and other close consultants were invaluable for feedback and encouragement: Mary Beach, Mo Dedrick, Suzanne Duval, Karen Smith, Leslie Brinson, and Molly Martin. In the brainstorming of titles, I think it was Mo who actually landed the final name, *Whispers for Terra*. I was equally honored by other professionals who continued to care, such as Donna Mazzitelli, and particularly my proofreader, Jennifer Jas, who helped me problem-solve final issues. My writer friends let me commiserate but kept me believing I could finish. Mo Dedrick said she'd be honored to have her photograph serve as the premise for the book cover. Claudia Edwards-Houser creatively designed my cover.

Most importantly, thanks to my amazing husband, Jon Bluhm, for living this journey every.single.day. for more than a year. For being okay with my head being in "book thought" probably too much of the time. For treading lightly with feedback when needed, and for stimulating creativity as only a Bluhm can do. I have loved you since that hopeful barbeque some thirty-plus years ago.

Notes

The author highly encourages readers to seek further information on the vital topic of soil. These are the sources (in random order) that guided and inspired her while writing this fictional story:

References for topics related to the Third Eye and dreams:

- Tanaaz, "How to Open and Activate Your Third Eye," Forever Conscious, foreverconscious.com.
- "5 Simple Techniques to Open Your Third Eye," chakras.info.
- Dr. Gerard C. Buffo, "The 3 Essential Steps to Open Your Third Eye," curejoy.com.
- Sivana East, blog.sivanaspirit.com.
- Rosemary Ellen Guiley, *Dreamwork for the Soul* (Berkley Books, 1998).
- Jeremy Taylor, *Where People Fly and Water Runs Uphill* (Grand Central Publishing, 1993).

References for topics related to soil:

- Radiolab, "From Tree to Shining Tree," 2016, wnycstudios.org.
- Suzanne Boothby, "Can Regenerative Agriculture Help Save the Planet?" *good4u Health Hotline Magazine*, April 2020, Natural Grocers, naturalgrocers.com.
- World Health Organization (WHO), who.int.
- Kristin Ohlson, *The Soil Will Save Us* (Rodale, 2014).
- Project Drawdown, drawdown.org.
- Alan Bojanic, Food and Agriculture Organization (FAO) representative in Brazil.

CPSIA information can be obtained
at www.ICGtesting.com
Printed in the USA
LVHW091425100621
689917LV00002B/10